"You are hurting Akeyla. Stop," I said. Jaxson Geroux was firmly entrenched inside his little nine-year-old alpha ditch and utterly unable to see that his hole wasn't a hill...."

WOLF HUNTED

NORTHERN CREATURES BOOK FOUR

KRIS AUSTEN RADCLIFFE

THE WORLDS OF
KRIS AUSTEN RADCLIFFE

Smart Urban Fantasy:

Northern Creatures

Monster Born

Vampire Cursed

Elf Raised

Wolf Hunted

Fae Touched

Death Kissed

God Forsaken

Magic Scorned (*coming soon*)

Genre-bending Science Fiction about
love, family, and dragons:

WORLD ON FIRE

Series one

Fate Fire Shifter Dragon

Games of Fate

Flux of Skin

Fifth of Blood

Bonds Broken & Silent

All But Human

Men and Beasts

The Burning World

Dragon's Fate and Other Stories

WOLF HUNTED

NORTHERN CREATURES
Book Four

By
Kris Austen Radcliffe

Six Talon Sign Fantasy & Futuristic Romance
Minneapolis

www.krisaustenradcliffe.com

Published by
Six Talon Sign Fantasy & Futuristic Romance

Edited by Annetta Ribken
Copyedited by Juli Lilly
"Northern Creatures" artwork created by Christina Rausch
Cover to be designed by Covers by Christian
Plus a special thanks to my Proofing Crew.

First print edition, January 2019
Version: 4.15.2021

ISBN: 978-1-939730-70-1

WOLF HUNTED

CHAPTER 1

The renewal of royal vows came as a surprise. Perhaps not to Alfheim's elves, or to her werewolves, but I was certainly caught off guard, mostly because I'd been busy since my return from Las Vegas. I had a woman to find.

A mysterious woman I could not remember. A woman who I suspected had my dog.

My canine emperor, Marcus Aurelius, was a stout hound of indeterminate breed, intelligent and fully capable of taking care of himself. He came home intermittently, mostly to say hello, looking well-fed and well-groomed and wagging his tail. Someone was caring for him.

But there would be no searching for either my dog or my mystery woman this afternoon. Not with a royal re-wedding to attend.

Ed Martinez, the currently-off-duty sheriff of our magical corner of the world, straightened his cufflinks and his tie. Like me, he wore a nice autumn-toned suit, his a warmish blue-gray flecked with gold that complemented his features, and mine a red-oak-tinted gray that warmed my otherwise sallow skin.

We were under orders to dress for the occasion, and had both been fitted by the town tailor, an elf with exquisite taste and an eye for proportion. Neither Ed nor I would have been nearly as well-coordinated if we'd been left to our own devices, though Ed at least understood where to shop and how to harmonize colors.

He looked up at my tie, frowned, and patted at the gray and maroon strip of fabric looped around my neck like a modern noose.

"How can you be two centuries old and not know how to tie a Windsor knot?" he asked.

I looked down at the tie. I often asked Maura to help because of my big, clumsy fingers, but she and Akeyla had already left by the time I'd returned from my daily—hourly, to be honest—venture into the woods surrounding my lake home.

She was out there somewhere, my mystery woman. Somewhere nearby. I swear I could feel her. So I looked every day.

Maura and Akeyla had noticed, and were beginning to make faces. Finding Marcus Aurelius worked as an excuse for about a week. Now both of my elven houseguests puckered their lips and tossed suspicious looks in my general direction every time I stepped off the deck and headed into the rustling trees.

"Frank," Ed said. "Focus."

I exhaled and looked up at the clear blue autumn sky over Alfheim. Arne Odinsson and Dagrun Tyrsdottir, our King and Queen, were about to renew their centuries-old marriage vows in Alfheim's downtown-adjacent tourist-filled Riverside Park, and they'd invited everyone—all the elves, wolves, townies, out-of-town tourists who'd come up from The Cities for the weekend, and every single one of the farmers in the surrounding territory. I was surprised we didn't have a senator or two, or the mayors of Bemidji, Brainerd, Duluth, and Grand Rapids here as well.

We didn't, as far as I could tell. The only politicians in the park were the local elves.

Ed adjusted my tie. I frowned and pulled on it myself. "It's fine."

He shook his head. "You're standing up with elves."

"So are you." Ed, Gerard Geroux—Remy was still in Las Vegas and would be home in a few days—one of the elven owners of Raven's Gaze Brewery and Pub, Bjorn Thorsson, and I were standing on Arne's side. Maura, Akeyla, Benta, and Axlam Geroux on Dag's side.

Someone had set up a video feed for Remy in Vegas; Magnus, who was in New Zealand; and a few other elves in other enclaves, whom I suspected were the real audience. After the International Conclave we'd all survived two weeks ago in Las Vegas, the other Elven Courts needed to be reminded that the King and Queen of Alfheim stood united.

At least this reminder had a bouncy castle for the kids.

How much time inside the giant forced-air wonder, complete with turrets and a unicorn, would the kids demand? If I left right after the ceremony, I could probably get in another hour or two of searching before Maura and Akeyla got home.

"Frank," Ed said as if reading my mind, "this post-Vegas obsession of yours isn't healthy."

Ed knew I was searching for someone. Every day, new surprise danced across his features when I asked for help. Then I got the bright idea to *not* ask and to offer a more mundane reason instead. Ed now thought I was looking for Marcus Aurelius. He remembered that there might be some sort of magical something-or-other involved, or a person, and when I had sheriff-actionable information, I'd share.

Besides, my "health" could weather most storms. We had a mystery woman trapped in concealment enchantments somewhere in Alfheim. What if she needed help? I needed to find her.

"Her name is Ellie Jones," I said. That much I knew.

One eyebrow arched. He was surprised I had a name, yet he still looked like a man about to crack a joke about invisible "Canadian girl-friends" stealing dogs.

Which, I suspected, was the work of the concealment enchantments. Ed was not a man who would ignore any information that might indicate someone needed help. Even if he wasn't an officer, he'd still be leading the volunteer squads doing sweeps.

I almost pulled out my phone. I almost showed him, yet again, the forlorn photo of Ellie and my wayward hound that always caught me off guard. How had the photo gotten onto my phone? Then my daily reminder appeared and I read the instructions from yet another mysterious woman named Chihiro Hatanaka, a Japanese woman enlisted by two kitsune to help me overcome the enchantments at the core of all my obsessive issues.

Ed never remembered the photo. I rarely did. Thankfully, I had Chihiro's list to help me overcome at least some of the forgetfulness.

But I had a name. I had a slightly sad photo of a beautiful woman with my dog. And I had a need.

Ed looked out over the hundreds of white chairs filling the open spaces under two of the park's larger oak trees. The area was usually used for band shelter seating. Instead of orienting the chairs to the east, where the shelter loomed over one corner of the park, the chairs had been oriented north, toward the trees.

Strong branches arched outward from both trees and mingled their rustling, reddish leaves. The elves had hung a partition of candles, ivy, apples, nuts, and fruits from the branches, sheltering a small tented area behind the trees. Arne and Dagrun would renew their vows in front of the elven bounty, among the chattering squirrels and the multitude of their friends and family.

The entire structure was autumn beauty at its finest.

Near the band shelter, an elf blew a horn. All the chatter stopped. People clasped hands and made their way to the seats.

It was time for Ed and me to find Gerard and Bjorn, and to take our places at the end of the aisle leading to the trees.

"Looks like we're up," Ed said.

I adjusted my cufflinks and straightened my tie yet again, then clasped his shoulder. "Come, my friend," I said, and walked toward our fellow groomsmen.

Bjorn Thorsson was a muscular, bear-like elf with extra-thick sideburns he never glamoured when he hid most of his also-extra-thick ponytail and his roundly pointed ears. He also stood eye-to-eye with Arne and Magnus, but carried enough width in his shoulders that he was almost as broad-chested as I.

He brewed up the best mead and craft beers in the state of Minnesota. Besides Alfheim's growing tourism industry and all of Magnus's business connections, we were becoming a foodie haven, and Bjorn's offerings at Raven's Gaze were a big part of why.

He also bred cats, mostly of the elf-approved Norwegian Forest variety; but he kept the foul-tempered Mr. Mole Rat, a tom of that gremlin-like hairless breed the name of which I could never remember, and the only cat on Earth that disliked my ex, Benta the Nameless.

I'd always suspected Bjorn was quite proud of Mr. Mole Rat. Hopefully that delight would not interfere with Arne and Dag's ceremony.

Bjorn stood at the end of the aisle between the chairs with his hands clasped behind his back and a stern-yet-approving look on his face. Like all the other elves, he'd glamoured away his most obvious magical characteristics. Bjorn, though, glamoured up shoulder-length black hair, which he pulled back into a mundane-worthy ponytail. I suspected he wore some Scandinavian hard rock band t-shirt under the suit, too.

Bjorn, like his cat, was what the kids these days called "metal."

Gerard, phone in hand, stood next to Bjorn, wearing a well-tailored gray suit like the rest of us. Jaxson knelt on the chair next to his father, his hands on the chair's back and his chin up so he could stare at Gerard's phone.

Jaxson pointed at the band shelter. "Mom and Akeyla will be out in a moment," he said. Maura and Benta must not be registering in his nine-year-old head, which was to be expected when the two most important women in his young life were out of his sight.

Gerard patted his shoulder and tucked away his phone. "Why don't you go up front and snag yourself a good seat with the pack?" He nodded toward the front and off to the side, where others of the Alfheim Pack, and Ed's family, gathered.

Jaxson, wide-eyed and looking overwhelmed, nodded once. He stood tall, straightened his button-front shirt in much the same way we all kept pulling on our cufflinks, and all but ran for the best seat in the house.

Gerard grinned as he watched his son go.

"I swear he grows an inch a month," Ed said.

Gerard's grin widened. "Axlam thinks he's going to be elf-height."

I didn't doubt it. The wolves tended to be correct in their predictions of children's growth, the weather, and just about anything contextual. Arne said it was wolf magic, but Gerard and Remy said it had more to do with fine-tuned wolf senses than anything magical.

"I'm surprised they did it this weekend," Bjorn said, "and not closer to Samhain."

Gerard shrugged. "Arne wanted the ceremony done before the feast and the full moon."

The full moon—and the wolf run—also fell on Samhain, and the night's magic also affected the werewolves. Samhain both intensified and thinned moon magic, and the wolves would be best protected with extra elves.

But there was nothing unusual about additional elves going out with the pack. Magical nights happened more frequently than not, and the elves had a routine set up, though the magic of the night often spread resources thin.

Gerard looked up at the sky. "We have a storm coming in." He sniffed. "First snow. Fifty bucks says it hits on Samhain."

Over a week out and Gerard could smell the forecast on the wind.

Bjorn nodded. "The moon and a blizzard. Exciting."

Gerard shrugged, then pointed toward the band shelter. "We're up, gentlemen."

Axlam, in a flowing red, gold, and green gown, stepped out of the shelter's staging area. She wore a matching headscarf dotted with a crown of autumn leaves and flowers, and she shimmered in the afternoon sunshine as much from the lovely fabrics of her dress as her innate wolf.

Mate magic flared off Gerard, and for a second, I thought he was about to bound across the park and carry away his wife. But he smiled instead, and a calm settled over his shoulders.

Axlam looked back into the shelter and extended her hand. Akeyla bounced out, her also-flowing dress more fiery than Axlam's, with her hair and ears wrapped and decorated in the same way. She took Axlam's hand and smiled at the crowd.

Maura and Benta followed, both with their glamour-hair braided and decorated with autumn florals, both in darker reds and purples that leaned more toward the cooler days of fall.

The women flowed across the park more than walked. Everyone quieted, and the chairs filled quickly and in an orderly fashion.

"Uncle Frank!" Akeyla looked as if she wanted to jump into my arms, but restrained herself and held out her small bouquet of sunflowers and crabapples. "Ready?"

Gerard and Axlam would walk first, then Akeyla and me, Ed and Benta, and Bjorn and Maura. Arne and Dag would say their renewal, and then the festivities would begin.

"Sure am, pumpkin," I said.

She bounced on her heels. "You're supposed to hold my hand." She transferred her bouquet to her free hand and grasped my fingers.

Up front, off to the side and under one of the trees, three elves strummed guitars and played flutes.

Maura patted my elbow. "Remember, sweetie," she said to Akeyla, "when you get up front, walk to Axlam. I'll be right behind you."

Akeyla nodded.

"You look fantastic," I said to Akeyla. "All of you," I said to the women.

Benta looked away. She smoothed her lovely dress over her lovelier hips and hooked her arm through Ed's. "It's quite the honor for a mundane to be called to stand for our King and Queen," she said.

Ed tossed me a *she's your girlfriend* look.

I scowled at Benta.

Akeyla bounced again. "Mr. Martinez isn't *mundane*. He's our *sheriff*," she said in classic Akeyla *don't be dumb* fashion.

No one looked at Benta except Akeyla, who obviously expected better from her grandmother's friend.

Ed took it in stride. Axlam and Maura looked proud. Bjorn, though, decided to be metal.

"I'm gonna need someone to look after Mr. Mole Rat next weekend, Benta. Interested?" He didn't look at her, but bowed slightly to Maura and offered his arm.

Gerard smirked, and when the music thankfully expanded into

our call to walk, he quickly took Axlam's arm and they made their way down the aisle between the chairs.

Akeyla smiled up at me, hooked her hand in mine, and strode out into the aisle with her Uncle Frank in tow. We parted and took up our places under the trees. Poor Ed, Benta with her arm hooked gingerly around his, followed, with Bjorn and Maura walking toward the trees last.

The music stopped. The elves set down their instruments and moved as a unit, two on either side, to draw back the partition.

Arne and Dag walked out of the tent behind the trees, Arne with his hands clasped behind his back, and Dagrun with hers clasped around her own small, autumn bouquet. They both glamoured minimally, hiding only their ears and elven hair from the guests in the chairs, and shimmered with their elven glory. Both wore tasteful, expensive clothes, Arne in a dark gray suit and Dagrun in a champagne-colored gown. She handed her bouquet to Maura and turned to her husband.

Arne's organic, deeper blue and purple magic swirled up into the air. Dag's icier, clockwork magic followed.

They clasped hands.

Words followed. Proclamations about love and life. Poetry about community and caring and family. Hands moved. Spells worked in ways that only the magicals in the audience understood.

Joyous fireworks danced among the swirls of magical color, and moved in waves between our King and Queen.

The sparks of mate magic swirled around Gerard and Axlam most of the time, and had recently begun flickering between Jaxson and Akeyla. In Las Vegas, I'd seen it move between Remy and his red-dressed nature-spirit mate, Portia Elizabeth. I'd always thought such magicks were wolf-centered.

Two hundred years in Alfheim and this was the first time I'd ever noticed mate magic moving between two elves—and two elves whose marriage had started as nothing other than a political alliance.

And never, in my two hundred years in Alfheim, had I seen Arne look at his wife with such concentration and reverence. I'd seen him use each separately—concentrating on her words or her movements, or with a reverent look of awe when he didn't realize he was being watched—but never both at the same time, and never in such a public setting.

Somewhere out in Alfheim was a concealed woman who I was sure deserved the same concentration and reverence. Deep down inside my enchantment-cocooned heart, I knew she was worthy of all the reverence my adopted father now gave my adopted mother.

I *knew*.

I had to find her. I had to, even if it was the last thing I did.

CHAPTER 2

Akeyla ran out of the women's restroom in the band shelter in full playwear—bright blue leggings, sneakers, and her prize "Alfheim Gossiping Squirrels" Sprout League t-shirt that Jax had given her after his team won regionals. She still had her hair and ears wrapped up in the scarf, but had removed most, though not all, of her decorative flowers.

"Uncle Frank! Mr. Bjorn!" She stopped a few feet from where we sat at one of the shelter's tables, and pointed at the massive, noisy bouncy castle not too far from the chairs. "Are you going to bounce?"

Seemed Arne had gone in with a few of the kids. Arne Odinsson, the King of the Alfheim Elves, had gone full town-father and was now bouncing around in the castle in his dress shirt and suit pants with half the town's school children.

Today was a day of wonders. "I think Bjorn and I are a bit big for bouncing," I said.

She shrugged. "Grandma said she'll bounce with me."

Bjorn looked as surprised by the play of his monarchs as I was. "I'm beginning to wonder if they came back from Las Vegas enchanted."

Akeyla looked over at the castle. "Where's Jax?"

I was surprised he hadn't been waiting while she changed. "I don't know," I said. "He's probably changing, too."

"Oh," she said. "I'm supposed to wait for Mommy." She sat on the bench next to Bjorn. "Can we get a kitten, Uncle Frank?"

Bjorn chuckled.

"Not until Marcus Aurelius comes home. We'll need his approval," I said.

She frowned, but didn't say anything else. Bjorn, either. They clammed up, which was very un-elf-like. But I had yet another gut feeling that the elves frowned and stopped asking questions when the topic got even peripherally close to my mystery woman. It made sense, with the concealment enchantments. I just wish I remembered well enough to fully recognize any day-to-day patterns.

Akeyla pointed off to the side of the bouncy castle. "Who's that?" she asked.

I turned around. Some smooth-looking guy I didn't recognize stood on the edge of the park, openly taking photos of the crowd with a big, obvious camera. "Did Arne and Dag hire a photographer?" I asked Bjorn.

He shook his head. "No. Only the video feed for the ceremony."

"That's an expensive camera he's wielding." I pointed. "That lens alone runs a good five grand." I'd priced photography equipment lately. Why, I couldn't remember, but I had a vague notion I'd been looking at buying a gift.

"Some of the most powerful witches use cameras as their seer stones. Some of them can read regular photos." Bjorn stood up. "We're not the only enclave with a 'no photography' policy unless the photographer is cleared by the elder elves."

I stood up, too.

We weren't the only ones to notice him. Ed, Gerard, and two other pack members had surrounded the guy before he could retreat to his car.

He raised his arms as if surrendering. Ed extended his hand. The guy handed over his camera.

"We're in a public space," I said. "I'm not sure anyone can stop him from taking photos." At least not without a little magical intervention. After what happened with my vampire brother and Akeyla at Lara's Café, I fully understood why none of the magicals in Alfheim wanted random mundanes photographing their lives.

"I don't like him," Akeyla said.

I looked down at my little niece. She stared at the guy with the camera, her face stern, and her hands balled into fists. Fire magic swirled around her in sheets of red and blue flames. Magic that was building into something strong enough it might manifest in a way noticeable by the mundanes.

"Can you tell us why, honey?" I asked.

Bjorn suddenly looked down at Akeyla. "It's okay," he said. "Sherriff Ed has it under control."

"No," she said.

I looked at Bjorn, who looked at me with just as much shock as I was sure I was showing. "Maura!" I called toward the shelter. Then to Bjorn, "Go. They need elf magic."

He jogged toward Ed and the wolves.

Ed opened the camera and took out the memory card. One of the other wolves ran toward Bjorn, nodded, and ran toward the bouncy castle, presumably to get Arne.

"He's a bad man, Uncle Frank," Akeyla said.

Axlam, Maura, and Dag exited the woman's restroom of the shelter. Dag immediately followed Bjorn toward the unknown man. Maura moved toward Akeyla and me. But Axlam stopped three feet from the door and stood unmoving as if she'd been frozen in ice.

Maura squatted and touched Akeyla's face. "Honey, what's wrong?" she said. She, too, had changed into something more bouncy-castle-worthy, as had Dag and Axlam.

Akeyla continued to stare at the bad man.

"Her magic's flaring," I said. "What's wrong with Axlam?"

Maura stood up. Gerard pushed the man, who threw up his hands again, and stepped back. Maura looked back at Axlam.

"Frank," she said, "what are you seeing?"

I see magic. The elves can't, nor can the wolves, and they long ago learned to trust my senses. "Akeyla's upset." I peered at the group of arguing men. "Bjorn and your mother are both in full protective mode." Sigils and spellwork geared and shifted around both of them. "Bjorn's put up a wall between the man and Ed, and Dag's clockwork magic looks like it's about to slam down on his head."

Maura pulled Akeyla close. "The wolves," she said.

Gerard's wolf magic flared as much as the elves'. It flowed off him, to his pack members, and back as if synchronizing the three men. "Nothing unusual," I said.

I looked at Axlam. She still stood three feet from the woman's restroom door. Her soft silk blouse and long skirt flowed around her body.

Her magic erupted as a wolf mirage that extended a good twelve feet in the air. Magic shot out from her, toward Gerard and her pack, and circled back, but unlike them, her wolf was just as present as her human form.

It sniffed and growled.

Gerard spun around and looked at his wife.

"The wolves sense something," I said. Something bad.

Ed handed the camera to Dag, now sans memory card. She rolled it around in her hands as if looking at it the way any mundane would, except she was wrapping it in some sort of spell, one that I suspected would keep it from working properly from now on.

The man's posture shifted to belligerent, then back to submissive as if he couldn't make up his mind what he wanted to do.

He took the camera, and held up his hands again, then pulled his wallet out of his pocket. What had to be business cards appeared, and he handed the wad to Ed, who picked them gingerly from his fingers as if they were poison ivy.

Dag pointed at the parking lot, and the man backed toward a nondescript sedan. When he looked over his shoulder, she dropped a tracer enchantment onto his back.

It slid off.

"Maura, your mother's tracer just slipped off his back."

"What?" she muttered. "That's not possible."

Ed read the name on the card. I couldn't hear, but his lips formed some long-winded phrase.

Gerard responded to Axlam's magic. He lunged at the now-running man, and would have caught him if his pack hadn't held him back.

Dag tossed a second tracer enchantment at the sedan. It, too, slid off.

Jax and Arne pushed their way through the crowd. Jax immediately ran toward Akeyla, but stopped and looked between his proto-mate and his mother.

Maura tugged on Akeyla's hand. "Let's go see if Axlam and Jax are okay," she said.

Akeyla blinked. She nodded, then ran toward Jax.

I reached for Maura's hand. "What just happened?" I asked.

She shook her head. "Did you see any magic around that man that would interfere with the tracers?"

"No," I said. "But from over here, the elf and wolf magic may have masked it."

She squeezed my hand. "Go tell Mom and Dad that whatever dark magic is at work, it's not obvious to you." Then she jogged toward the kids, who were now both hugging Axlam.

Arne waved me over. I nodded, then looked back at Axlam. She stood tall with the same strong, stoic poise in which she always carried herself. The same poise every strong woman who had ever been, or continued to be, hounded by evil carried. Axlam Geroux, Alpha of the Alfheim Pack, was not a stranger to harm.

She held the kids against her sides, but reached for Maura's hand.

Something sinister had just walked into Alfheim. Something that, unlike my brother, didn't feel the need to slither around in the shadows. This sinister showed up at the reaffirmation of vows and destroyed the goodwill of the community just as effectively as popping the bouncy castle.

I walked toward the elves and wolves. Time to stand up, once again, for my King and Queen—and Alfheim.

14

CHAPTER 3

Gerard jogged by as I walked toward the knot of wolves and elves on the edge of the parking lot.

"What—" I started to ask, until he held up his hand.

His honey-colored eyes shimmered. His wolf was closer to the surface than it should be with all the mundanes around. "Ask Arne," he said, and continued toward his wife and son.

Bjorn was tapping at his phone when I walked up, and only nodded. Ed stood apart from the other men, his hands on his hips and his eyes narrow, as he stared in the direction in which the photographer had driven away. The pack dispersed—mostly, I suspected, to inform and to rally.

Arne pinched the memory card between his thumb and forefinger and held it pointing downward as if the little bit of plastic and circuitry was some sort of magical tome. Dag, who stood at a forty-five degree angle to her husband, cupped her hand under the card, but did not physically touch it.

Magic coiled off Arne's arm and around the card just as a matching magic coiled upward from Dag.

"I feel no magic here," Arne said.

"Nor do I," Dag answered.

Dag's hand fell away. Arne motioned to me. He dropped the card onto my palm. "Do you see anything?"

I rolled it around in my hand, then pinched it the same way Arne had, and peered closely at its surface. "I saw your tracers slide off both him and his car, by the way." I glanced out at the parking lot. "Don't see them now."

Dag swept her hand through the air and both tracers materialized over her palm. She rolled over her arms and flicked them back into place just above her wrists. "I sensed no counter-spell."

Arne and Dag's elf magic clung to the plastic and the metal connectors of the memory card. I squinted and flipped it over and peered at it edge-on.

"There's a shadow." *Something* clung to the card, or had at one time. "I can't tell if it's a remnant of removed magic or if there's something else here."

Arne frowned. "He obviously wasn't as mundane as we thought." He held out the man's business card.

Tom Wilson Photography, it said. *Weddings, engagements, and scenic photos*, and an address.

"Why is a Bemidji photographer in Alfheim?" I asked. Especially one so slick magic didn't cling to him.

"He said that he'd been hired by a corporation to document Northern Minnesota," Bjorn said. "Said the images were for brochures. He's been 'documenting' now for over a year."

"How strange," I said.

Bjorn held up his hand. "Found his benefactor." He held up his phone. "Natural Living Incorporated." He looked up from his screen.

Ed stared at the crowd, and specifically at the kids—his included—who chased each other around the bouncy castle. "He was lying." He nodded toward the oak trees. "And excited like a kid making one of those stupid Internet prank videos."

Arne frowned as if he didn't understand Ed's reference.

Ed shrugged. "My oldest watched a couple of pranksters for a while until he got bored. Said all the lying and flashy stupidity made the boys doing the pranks look desperate for attention." He nodded toward the road. "The photographer seemed desperate like that."

The last thing we needed was a team of dumb kids thinking they could make a small town look stupid by strapping a rocket to a shopping cart and sending it down Main Street. Or worse, by groping the locals.

"None of you read magic on him?" I asked.

Dag shook her head. "The pack reacted. Gerard and the others didn't sense anything specific, but they're sure they sensed a darkness."

And her tracers had slid off. "Then the shadow around the card probably is some sort of concealment enchantment," I said.

A mundane prank, this was not.

Arne stared off in the distance in much the same way as Ed. "He may have no idea he carries the magic."

Dag nodded. "Like Maura's ex's island magic, it might be something creepily persistent."

The elves looked at each other in turn, all three of them with strained, unhappy faces.

I was unaccustomed to the elven paralysis. Any magic, no matter how shadowy or creepily persistent, was to be rooted out and disposed of posthaste. Yet here stood our King and Queen on the edge between the park's green grass and the lot's black tar, both with their hackles up, but neither knowing where to punch.

Perhaps this "shadow" caused the same response as the concealments around my mystery woman.

"Lennart says he'll check the card." Bjorn held out his phone again. "By the way, Frank, your satchel is ready."

That meant Lennart had finished the stasis pouch I'd commissioned to hold Rose's notebook. The elder elf who had made Remy's pouches for his sketchbooks was long dead, and both Arne and Dag were busy. I figured Lennart would enjoy the challenge, and the opportunity to engage in some precise magic.

"Great." I said. "I'll head over."

Arne handed the card to Bjorn. "Tell Lennart thank you, and that we missed him today."

Bjorn's lips pinched. "I told him that there were plenty of elves here who would sit with him. He said he didn't want to be a distraction."

Lennart was one of Alfheim's most magically powerful—and magically overwhelmed—elves. Any elf who took their own name so young, as Lennart had in his early twenties, only did so because his magic demanded it of him. And Lennart's magic was prominent, powerful, and as bombastic as his namesake.

Where Bjorn walked the world more as the "elf of the common man" part of his namesake's magic, Lennart was all storms, all the time.

He didn't get out much, mostly because even with all his power, he had a difficult time holding a glamour. Sadly, he spent most of his time hiding in the back of Raven's Gaze Brewery with Mr. Mole Rat and Bjorn's other cats.

Arne sighed. They'd been through this with Lennart many, many times. They all seemed as continually surprised by his polite lack of confidence as I was, considering his Thor-like magic. But then again, I knew nothing of his past, or why he'd come to Alfheim in the first place. Like so many of us, he was another stray taken in by Arne and Dag.

"We will investigate when things wind down here," Arne said.

Ed returned to staring at the lot's exit. He wasn't any better at disguising his body language than our guest had been. Ed's hackles were up even more so than the elves'. He scratched his cheek. "I don't want any problems with the pack," he said. "The last thing Alfheim needs is close to thirty angry, wild-with-Samhain werewolves going into a full moon."

I looked back at the band shelter. Gerard stood protectively between his family and the lot. Axlam continued to hold Jax against her side. Akeyla had moved to Maura, but held tight to Jax's hand.

"We need to figure this out," I said. Now, before the wolves whipped themselves into a frenzy.

Dag squeezed my arm again, then took Arne's hand. They walked toward Gerard.

Bjorn tucked his phone into his pocket. "I told Lennart I'd be home in an hour or two." Then he, too, walked back toward the festivities.

Ed returned to staring at the road. "Do me a favor," he said.

"Anything," I answered.

He didn't turn around. He didn't flinch or fidget. But his shoulders visibly tightened under his jacket. He slowly exhaled. "Remind Arne that I brought my family here because he told me his town and its magic would keep my kids safe."

Arne had yet to grant Ed access to The Great Hall. Most of the time when a threat came around, Arne sent the Martinez family to the Alfheim Pack for protection. One of Ed's deputies was pack—two now, with Mark Ellis joining the force—so I suspected Arne thought Ed would be more comfortable in Gerard and Axlam's warded and spell-protected home with his mundane-trained law enforcement.

I rubbed my ear. I shouldn't make excuses for the elves. No matter how much I loved the family who'd adopted me, they were still elves, and they had their elven issues.

"I will." How was I to explain to Arne that he needed to take a long, modern look at his motivations? Maybe Maura could help.

Ed sniffed, as if getting a whiff of the words we spoke would give him some deeper understanding than listening alone. "At least this time we know there's something hidden here."

"I did see a shadow," I said.

He pulled his ever-present notebook from his pocket. "I'm going to do some digging on Natural Living Incorporated, the old-fashioned way." Ed gripped my elbow. "Thank you." Then he, too, walked away.

I pulled out my phone to text Lennart and let him know I was on my way over. I swiped… and looked down at the photo of my mystery woman.

Damn it, I thought. Whatever clung to the photographer wasn't the only concealment I was dealing with. At least the new magic wasn't slipping out of my mind the way she was.

I touched her face. *Her name is Ellie*, I thought. *Ellie Jones.*

Too many mysteries polluted my life. I tucked away my phone. I needed to find her, and I would. If I happened to be a few hours late to Raven's Gaze, what would it hurt?

CHAPTER 4

R aven's Gaze Brewery and Pub occupied two older buildings between Wolftown and the artsy neighborhood around the college. Like every place where elves live, the greenery here was lush, and the animals fat and happy. Massive trees shaded the tables and seating in front of the building's old brick façade, and kitchen gardens filled most of the space between the eatery and the brewery proper.

Raven's Gaze Brewery and Pub had been painted diagonally across the front of the eatery along with the unironic *established 1062, Alfheim, Minnesota*. The entire design was obvious from the road with its worn, rustic colors and conspiracy of navy blue raven silhouettes. Several of the tables were shaded by wide umbrellas printed with the same birds.

The pub and brewery would not have been out of place in Minneapolis's trendier neighborhoods. But the buildings weren't in The Cities; they were here with the elves. The pub still tended to be busy most evenings.

Neither Bjorn nor Lennart ran the restaurant. That fell to a rotating crew of mundane managers, all of whom seemed to do a decent job, but one of the cooks was an elf. The food was excellent, and they did deliver all the way out to my lake, beer included.

Between Lara's Café, Raven's Gaze, and the handful of other restaurants in town, Alfheim kept the tourists happy.

I parked Bloodyhood in the back of the pub's lot, away from the other cars and where my truck's brand-new plow attachment wouldn't scuff or be scuffed. Bloodyhood was one of the bigger models available anyway, which I needed because of my size, and with the plow, she pretty much took up two end-to-end spots.

Sal hummed to herself in her magazine pocket on the back of the passenger seat. She had her own special slot in my truck's toolbox, but she preferred to ride in the cab, and since she asked nicely, I wasn't going to say no. She glamoured her handle so she looked like an old, worn, wood-chopping axe, and put off waves of *leave me alone* that also served to keep people away from my truck.

My axe was a better deterrent than the truck's anti-theft systems.

"I'm going to walk around the neighborhood," I said.

My mighty elven battle axe tossed me a clear *You're searching for your mystery again, aren't you?*

Sal didn't so much talk as toss me comprehension. I didn't hear her per se, but I knew what she wanted me to know.

"Of course I am," I said.

She *humphed*. She wanted a stroll.

"I can't walk around with you on my shoulder. There are tourists."

She *humphed* again.

"I'll take you with me this evening. We'll walk around the lake."

Sal reluctantly agreed to my compromise, but didn't fully believe I'd stick to my word.

"I promise," I said.

She axe-sighed, which involved a subdued flash of purple-ish magic.

I shook my head. "You're testy today." She must have picked up on the activity at the park. "We have the situation under control. No need to worry."

A renewed flash of desire to walk the neighborhood followed.

I looked out at the big oaks in front of Raven's Gaze, and the remaining autumn blooms in the plantings in front of the restaurant.

A few tourists sat at the tables drinking brews. Two more people, both with cameras, stood staring at a guidebook on the walk down the street. They pointed at the large historic former church on the other side of a stand of trees. The building was visible from the restaurant parking lot, but not so much from the restaurant itself. The couple nodded and chatted, and one took several photos.

Bjorn owned the old church. There were "plans." What those plans were, I didn't know. But the building had a soft magical shimmer that made it more interesting than it would be otherwise.

The elves never stopped the tourists from taking photos within Alfheim. But then again, they'd also built in enchantments that kept the tourist photos to certain areas, like the church.

I pulled open my door. "I'll be back in a bit," I said. I still wore my dress shirt, slacks, and shoes, so I wouldn't be doing anything other than strolling, anyway.

My axe stayed silent this time.

I fiddled with my jacket, which I'd tossed onto the passenger seat, and pulled my wallet from the pocket.

I locked the truck and walked toward the church. How many times had I checked this part of town? Had I made a list? I opened my phone's notetaking app and looked.

Chihiro Hatanaka's list popped up.

Associate memories tangentially, item one said. The less a memory was connected directly to Ellie Jones, the more likely I was to remember it. The sub-notes said to try this with Ed, which I obviously had at one point or another.

The second item said to make notes about my activities, and to keep as many of those notes as possible on my person, and to back up to a cloud server before sundown. I checked; my phone did so automatically.

I was also to text Chihiro with regular updates, and to never give up.

Ellie Jones was here, somewhere. Even if she didn't want to be found, or if she didn't want to talk to me, I could at least give her Chihiro's contact information.

Something told me that connecting them was as important as anything I had to say.

I tapped my screen and filled in a note with the date, time, and location of this search, then tucked the phone back into my pocket. Checking around the church wouldn't take much time.

The two tourists were chatting excitedly as they walked toward Raven's Gaze. They both shot me the usual shocked looks people give anyone taller than six-five. Both mouths rounded momentarily, and the man did the also-usual look-down-and-to-the-right as he tried to place me in the pantheon of famous sports stars.

This was another reason I preferred living in Alfheim than, say, The Cities. Here, no one stopped me in the street and asked which team I played for.

Though being mistaken for a professional athlete was a world's worth of preferable to the terrified screaming of my unholy "youth."

"Howdy." I smiled and tipped my head as a friendly gesture.

The woman smiled back. The man did not. I walked on by.

The church wasn't large, and sat about fifty people while in use. It dated from the city's official incorporation just after Minnesota's statehood, and would have fallen into complete decay if the elves hadn't seen fit to preserve it. Or, more precisely, Bjorn.

Standing in front of the building, it was clear why.

I'd long wondered if the presence of Nordic elves in Northern Minnesota was why so many Norwegian, Swedish, and Icelandic immigrants settled here. If, somehow, they were drawn to their elves and their old gods.

The church had been built by some of the first immigrants who had found Arne's town. Bjorn had long lived on these lands, and he was a personable elf, even with his enjoyment of fast, loud music. And the immigrants, being Norwegians, probably understood they were in the presence of a being of Thor.

The wooden church, though filled with Christian imagery, was a beautiful temple to the thunder god, with its skyward-pointed A-line architecture, its many stories, its clear Viking longboat beams, and its stout, strong pillars carved with Norse designs.

Alfheim was blessed to have it.

"Is the tattoo on your neck the same as the design on the door of the church?"

I blinked and looked down. I hadn't heard the man approach. He stood behind me and off my elbow, a smallish man at least fifteen inches shorter than my almost seven feet. He wore an expensive dress shirt and slacks not all that different from my own yet-more-practical clothes.

His expensively cut hair had also been expensively styled. His cuff-links sparkled in the afternoon sun. His shoes looked to have cost about the same as Bloodyhood.

Yet he looked familiar, even if he wasn't carrying a camera or other gear and had put on the expensive jacket. "You're the photographer," I said.

The man shrugged and pointed at my Yggdrasil tattoo. "The tree. On the door." He pointed at the church.

He wore the top button of his shirt undone and a thin-yet-obvious gold chain around his neck. A big gold insignia ring adorned his pinkie. Not even Magnus walked around in such cliché rich-man attire.

"Maybe," I said. I stuck out my hand. "Frank. Why are you still in town?"

He carried no obvious magic. He also sneered at my hand as if I carried Ebola.

He shook it anyway. "Perhaps I like the amenities. Perhaps I want my memory card back." He waved his hand as if the card didn't matter. "Perhaps I'd like a burger." He nodded toward Raven's Gaze.

No accent colored his voice. Not even the ever-so-slight Cities cadence, or the lilt common in most of the small towns in the area. Nothing in the way he spoke suggested New Jersey, or Los Angeles, or Chicago. If anything, the gaudy display of wealth screamed European organized crime.

"*Hmmm*," I said, as if agreeing.

"It's lovely work," he said. "The tattoo. Is it from the local shop? The one downtown?"

A rich man—too rich to be a local photographer—was asking about my tattoos. "Yes," I said. *Close enough*, I thought.

"Ah." He clasped his hands behind his back and returned to staring at the church. "I swear some of these churches were built for the true gods. Don't you agree?"

Was he poking, trying to find a magic hole? At the park, he'd acted as if surprised by local disapproval. Nothing in his voice communicated that he had an ulterior motive. He sounded sincere in his question of immigrant motives.

Sincere, yes, but not compassionate. He sounded bored.

"I wouldn't know," I said.

"Yggdrasil, correct? The tree of life brings magic to every place it roots." He swept his hand through the air. "Magic built on the backs of the people who extend their hands and offer help."

"What was your name again?" Bjorn had said Tom something.

The sun dipped behind a cloud and his lack-of-magic… changed. Solidified, perhaps. And what hadn't been there to begin with became a shadow that could swallow the moon.

My instincts said to put him in a headlock and call for magical help, but he'd have an expensive lawyer here lawyering me into aggravated assault charges.

Better to pull as much info from him as I could.

I turned fully toward him. I spent most of my life trying not to physically intimidate anyone. Today, intimidation was necessary.

The open area in front of Raven's Gaze came into view.

There she was, my mystery woman, no more than twenty feet away.

CHAPTER 5

I rarely cursed magic. There was no point. Magic was a force of nature, and like all forces of nature, it cared nothing for the people, places, and things over which it steamrolled.

Some magic wielders, on the other hand, could be cursed all the way to Hell. And whoever wove the concealment enchantments around the woman twenty feet away could rot in the most debased pits in all the versions of The Land of the Dead.

I wanted to call her name. I tried, but it wouldn't come out. "Hey!" I shouted instead.

She was the most beautiful woman I had ever seen. Benta had her feline allure, but for all her expertise with spellwork, organization, and love of the natural world, she was still Benta.

Auburn fire danced in Ellie's hair where the dappled afternoon sun crossed her hoodie. She smoothed her hands over the thighs of her jeans, then jammed them into the big pocket on the front of her sweatshirt.

She tugged on the strap of her backpack, and looked over her shoulder.

The pack's pocket came into view—as did the stain along the

zipper. A stain I recognized. Ellie Jones wore my pack on her back. *My* pack. Somehow, some time, I'd given her my bag.

When? Where? How many times had we done exactly what we were doing right now?

Her lips rounded. She blinked. And I swore she said my name.

"Hey!" I called again.

The interloper stepped around me, as if my interruption of his subtext-laden questions was a crime worthy of a kick in the gut. "Who are you—"

I refused to look down at his weasel-like face. "I am no longer speaking to you," I said.

His head swiveled and he looked in Ellie's direction, but frowned and blinked as if he didn't see her. "You are Frank Victorsson," he said.

He knew my full name.

I glared down at the little man standing between Ellie and me. He had the angular features and the brown eyes I associated with French heritage, and carried an echo of the Geroux brothers. But mostly what I saw was his Mafioso-style bravado.

Ellie glanced wide-eyed at me again, and I swear she hiccupped. Her hand extended toward me just a fraction of an inch, but she pulled it back.

She turned away.

"Wait!" I called. "Please!"

The interloper gripped my forearm. "Victorsson," he said, clearly accentuating his lack of *Mister* in his words, "The leaders of this town need discipline."

He was just a mundane. He carried no obvious magic. Causing him pain would be too easy. "Remove your hand from my arm," I growled.

He let go, but did not step back. "*You* need discipline."

Ellie stared at the interloper. Her expression hardened. She took a step toward us.

I shook my head *no*. She couldn't come near this man. He might not be magical, but he was up to something, and I couldn't risk his darkness interacting with her enchantments.

A loud truck full of local kids pulled into the Raven's Gaze parking lot, followed by a second vehicle full of more kids. They tumbled out, laughing and touching like teenagers do, and moved toward the pub.

Ellie looked at the vehicles. She looked back at me. Then she ran into the trees between the church and restaurant.

"Damn it!" Without thinking—without considering the danger touching a rich man might bring—I gripped the interloper's shoulders. I lifted. And before he could squirm or yell or threaten, I set him to the side.

I should call Arne. I should let the elves know that the annoying photographer with the terrible attitude had shown up at Raven's Gaze. Or I could follow Ellie.

I ran for the trees.

"Come back!" I yelled. Why did she run away? I rushed toward the church, and rounded the building into a patch of buckthorn. Leaves drifted down from the ash and oak, and I could make out the brightly colored umbrellas covering the outdoor tables at Raven's Gaze, but Ellie had vanished.

"I have..." I yelled. I had something for her. "I'm trying!" Damn it, where did she go? I peered through the underbrush. "Ellie!" I finally got out her name.

"Frank."

I whipped around. Ellie stood next to the church, under a carving of a saint that looked more Norse god than godly. She adjusted the straps of the backpack and sighed deeply but didn't reach for me.

I pushed my way through the brambles. "I remember your name," I said.

The sigh turned into a slight quiver of her lower lip. "You remember that someone else told you my name," she said.

"Yes, that's true." I stepped out of the brambles and extended my hand. "I'm trying to circumvent the enchantments."

She pointed at my leg. "You ruined your pants."

I looked down. I'd ripped a small hole in the thigh of my trousers pushing through the undergrowth. "Oh." I patted at the hole as if my fingers would brush it away.

The interloper trotted down the path back toward the church. I moved to step between him and Ellie, but she put her finger to her lips and stepped in front of me.

The man peered into a window, then out into the trees. He walked toward us, stopped about seven feet away, and scowled.

Ellie was hiding me from him, and I'd ruined his good day by vanishing before he'd finished his insults.

He snapped a fingernail across the inside of his ring's band, swore, and walked away.

She stared toward the parking lot for what felt like forever. "He's magical, Frank. He couldn't see me." She jammed her hands into her hoodie's pocket. "The concealment enchantments hide me from other magicals." She stepped closer. "They hide you, too, when you're close enough."

Close like now. I could touch her elbow, or her hip. I could feel her skin.

Ellie adjusted the pack again. "He carries elf-level magicks. Please be careful around him. *Please.*"

Loneliness radiated from her like a cold heat. Or maybe it radiated off me and she was only reflecting a truth I'd been living for two centuries. But it was there in the set of her shoulders and the small steps toward me, then back, then toward me again.

Her concealments didn't hide dark magic the way the interloper's had. Hers turned her into a ghost with no moorings.

I reached for her. I had to. She couldn't hurt like this. Not my Ellie.

She stepped into my embrace. She curled her arms around my waist. And the woman who lived her life behind a veil laid her head against my chest.

She pressed against my front as if holding on for dear life.

Nothing else mattered. Not our interloper. Not the coming blizzard. Not the elves or the damned town or Samhain or anything else. She touched me and the hurts of my life—all the pain and the conflict and the anger—it all vanished. It fell away, and I knew why I'd made the decades of effort necessary to leave it behind. I understood why I'd worked so hard to not be the monster my father built.

"I miss you so much," she said.

She wasn't a ghost, nor was she a phantom or a dream. Her heart beat against my chest. Her warmth touched my skin, and her breath my soul.

And I'd found her... again. What was I forgetting? She missed me. She hugged me. We had a relationship. We did. The proof clung to me now. Ellie Jones was more than a woman who needed help. She was more than a friend.

A tsunami-like need to protect burst upward from my gut and into my throat. It moved outward into my limbs and pulled Ellie even closer.

"Chihiro said that I need to acclimate the enchantments to my presence. I have a list on my phone." I'd get Ellie through the conceal-ments—or I'd find a way in.

She pulled back. "You talked to Chihiro?" A spark flickered across her face.

She was surprised.

"Yes," I said. "She remembers you. I made a deal with two kitsune while in Las Vegas. They found her and added her number to my phone." I pulled my phone out of my pocket.

"You shouldn't have made a deal with kitsune, Frank," she said.

I shrugged. "I ended up making a lot of deals in Las Vegas I prob-ably shouldn't have." I held out my phone so she could see. "It was worth it."

Her finger floated over the screen for a split second, until she gently touched Chihiro's phone number. "Is she okay?" Her lip quiv-ered more now than it had before. "When my cottage moved, it hurt her." She pulled back her hand. "It hurt me, too."

Her concealment moved her cottage? How was that possible? And when it moved, it harmed Chihiro, and it harmed Ellie.

She touched my cheek. "My home doesn't mean to hurt anyone. It gives plenty of warning before a move, so I can take precautions." She touched my phone again. "Chihiro is stubborn."

For a split second, I was sure she thought the magicks that moved her cottage were about to reach out and do to me what they did to Chihiro.

31

"She hasn't said anything about injuries," I said.

Ellie sniffed and rubbed at her eyes. "I don't have any way to call her," Ellie whispered.

"I'll get you a phone." I pointed at the parking lot. "We can go right now. I'll put you on my plan."

A small, pinched grin moved across Ellie's lips. She chuckled once, and shook her head.

"We've done this before," I said.

Ellie gently touched my forearm. Her fingers, separated from my skin by the fabric of my dress shirt, moved downward toward my wrist.

She was an inch from taking my hand. Inches from accepting what I offered. An inch from returning to my embrace and admitting she didn't have to face her enchantments alone.

I was caught in that inch. Me, the "giant" of Alfheim, was trapped in that miniscule space between her walking away and me giving her all I had.

I needed her to let me help. I needed to show her win after win, even if they were small and incremental. I needed her to acknowledge that tiny little space, to roll up her sleeves, and get to work building it out with me.

Her concealments might make my mind forget, but right now, with her almost taking my hand, I was pretty sure they couldn't stop my body's memory. Every individual cobbled-together piece of me knew the truth of my emotions.

Her fingers stopped at the cuff of my dress shirt. "I lost the last phone you gave me when we were dealing with the vampires."

What *was* I forgetting? Was her reluctance to take my hand because of something that happened with vampires? Was it something I did?

She chuckled. "Do you still have my bike?" She lifted her hand off my arm. Just like that, she broke the connection. She severed our tether and now I drowned in the bottom of the deep, small space between us.

"Ellie." I reached for her again.

She clasped my hands, but did not return to my arms. She clasped them to hold the space between us. "My green bike."

Please don't hold me away, I thought. I almost spoke those five words. I probably should have. But frightening her would have slashed much deeper than her requesting space.

"The bike I found," I said. "It's yours? It's in my garage. I haven't had time to fix it." I didn't know *why* I wanted to fix it, either. Now I did.

"I need some way to get around."

"I'll get your bike fixed," I said. "It's going to snow soon." I pointed at the sky. "A bike won't do. You'll need a vehicle."

She looked away and didn't answer.

"Ellie," I said. "I'll get you whatever you need. I'll buy a car and leave the keys for you. All you have to do is ask."

She frowned and the space between us grew wider. She stepped back, and that space became a gulf.

So I changed the subject. "The wolves say we have a blizzard coming in on the evening of Samhain," I said, hoping to pull her attention back to building our space instead of allowing it to crush us.

"That's terrible timing," she said.

"It is." I'd distracted her from leaving. "Especially since we have an interloper. The wolves sensed some sort of dark magic at the park today when the guy showed up the first time." I pointed back at the walk. "The elves didn't sense anything, but I saw a shadow."

She spun around and pointed at the small fence separating the walk from the brambles. She squeezed my fingers. "When your brother kidnapped you, we used my ability to hide from other magicals to save Benta."

Her hand twitched. She let go and looked away again.

Benta had stayed the night after we returned from Vampland.

My stomach soured. And once again I realized that even if my mind forgot, my body did not.

I'd unintentionally hurt Ellie by allowing Benta to stay.

"I'm sorry." I reached for her again. "I didn't know. It won't happen again."

No surprise registered on her face, just resignation. "Frank..."

I stepped to her and pulled her into my arms. I kissed her hair. Such intimacy was presumptuous, especially now, with a Benta-shaped wraith between us. But I wasn't going to give up without a fight. "I promise."

She pulled away. "You said the same thing when you picked up my bike." Her lip quivered again.

I swiped open my notes. "I'll write this down. All of it, Ellie. Even if I don't consciously remember, part of me knows. I'll follow Chihiro's instructions. Your enchantments are going to see me as part of your world. I *promise*." I just needed to be on the inside.

That was the key. It *had* to be the key. I needed to get inside the enchantments. Chihiro had. She got in and the enchantments stopped messing with her memory.

And Chihiro wasn't the only one to get in.

"You have my dog," I said.

She nodded. "I don't bring him into town. I don't want questions from mundanes who know he's yours."

"He got inside the enchantments. He comes to visit me every couple of days, then he leaves again on his own. He remembers you, and he always returns."

Her brow knitted, and her mouth rounded. "I didn't realize."

"I think the enchantments don't want you to realize. Because once you realize, *you* can pick and choose who comes in, and not the magic."

Ellie straightened the backpack and looked up at the sky. "What if figuring out how to circumvent the enchantments is what triggers the magic that moves my cottage? It caused Chihiro agony. What if it does the same thing to you?" She looked up at the sky. "I can't do this, Frank. I can't find a way to be with you and then have you ripped away from me."

"We don't know if that will happen. Chihiro remembers you. We don't—"

"I'll shatter." She ran toward the parking lot.

I'm big and I'm fast. I scooped her up before she got too far. I lifted her into the air and buried my face against her neck. "Let me try. Please, Ellie. Please," I whispered.

Ellie wailed but she held on.

I'd fallen into this moment as if it was a magical pocket land. I had no past here, and only scant understanding of its rules. But I knew it would slam closed soon, and I'd lose her tears on my shoulder. I'd lose her arms around my chest and the feel of her hair against my neck.

I was head over heels in love with a magical woman whom I could only touch when the magic ignored us both.

"Frank!" someone called from the restaurant side of the trees. "Hey, Frank, you in there?"

Ellie pushed on my shoulders. "Put me down."

"No." I'd vowed long ago that I would never disrespect a woman's wishes. But this was different. I would only comply with the side of her ambivalence I supported.

"Frank..." Ellie cupped my cheeks, and she kissed me with more passion than I'd ever felt from another woman. She wrapped her arms around my head and she kissed me as if this was the last time we would ever see each other.

I curled my fingers into her hair. "Please, Ellie," I whispered.

"Frank?" the voice called again.

The defeat in Ellie's sigh played across my lips and chin. Gently, she removed my hand from her hair, and just as gently, she kissed my fingers.

I was about to lose her again. *Again.* "No, no, Ellie, please," I whispered. "Don't go."

She nodded toward the voice. "What's the elf's name?"

"Lennart," I said. "He's a good guy. He'll help." He would. All the elves would. She just needed to let me figure out how to make it happen.

She laid her forehead against my cheek. "He can't." Then she wiggled out of my embrace and ran down the path toward the parking lot.

Lennart popped through the brush.

I looked up at the elf who couldn't see Ellie running away. I looked back as she vanished around the corner.

I wanted to yell out her name. I wanted to follow.

But Lennart put his hand on my shoulder. "Come on. Your satchel's ready," he said.

Ellie's concealments screamed like a gang of terrified meerkats at the elf standing next to me. They screamed and they threw up their barriers.

And once again, the most important person in my life slipped away.

CHAPTER 6

Ellie disappeared into the thick trees beyond the church with her hands buried in her hoodie's pocket and my backpack on her back. Gone, like a ghost. She vanished as if her enchantments refused to allow me to see her anymore.

My fist balled. My arm rose. The muscles of my back and arm tightened to throw every joule of my energy into a carved saint whose only mistake was to scowl down at the mundanes below.

"Hey!" Lennart caught my wrist. He'd come through the brush and onto the path around the church with hardly a sound. "No punching churches."

He was larger than most of the other elves, with wider-than-average shoulders and a more prominent upper body than either Arne or Magnus. Lennart was overall thinner than the bear-like Bjorn, though, and looked like a rock star.

He was also one of the few elves strong enough to give me pause.

"Let go," I said.

Lennart let go of my wrist. He stepped back, but held his arm ready in case he needed to catch another swing. "I saw your truck." He pointed at the lot. "Are you okay?" He pointed at the spot on the church wall I was about to punch.

I wanted to tell him that Ellie ran away. I wanted him to whip up one of his stormy spells and send forth his thunder to find her enchantments. But no words left my mouth.

The confused look all the elves got when their questions got too close to Ellie manifested. He rubbed at the hat over his ears.

Lennart didn't glamour his extra-thick sideburns, nor did he hide the lines of his elven tattoos much, and they shimmered in the late afternoon sun. Like Bjorn, Lennart leaned toward metal, and seldom wore anything other than black. Even the hunting leathers he wore while running with the wolves were solid black with only a few silver studs.

Today he wore a black t-shirt, black jeans, forearm-covering black leather bracers, and a white knit cap. Under the hat, his ears were as unglamoured as his sideburns and made owl-like points that framed the big gold and maroon University of Minnesota Duluth bulldog right in the middle of his forehead.

Ellie, I thought. Where did she go? She'd run away. And...

She'd kissed me. And now Lennart's elf-ness interacted with her concealments and I didn't know what do to.

She'd *kissed* me.

"You look like you saw a ghost," Lennart said. He peered at the church behind us. "Not a literal ghost, I hope."

My girlfriend had just vanished again and he wanted to talk about ghosts? Once again, no words about enchantments, or Ellie, or ghosts left my throat.

I swore under my breath and swiped open my phone.

"Why don't you come in." Lennart pointed over his shoulder. "You can look at your messages while I get your satchel."

I'm not looking at messages, I thought. I tried to tap in notes about Ellie, but I couldn't. No symbol on my phone looked like a symbol, even though they did. Nothing made sense, the way typing and reading and words make no sense in dreams.

I swore again and tucked my phone into my pocket.

"Fine," I said. Hopefully I'd remember enough once I was out of Lennart's orbit to add notes to my list. But...

She needed a phone. Chihiro said to associate memories tangentially. "How many lines does your phone plan have?" I asked.

Lennart shrugged. "Five, I think. Why?"

How was I supposed to answer that question? My invisible girlfriend needs a means of communication? "Ghosts," I said.

The elf standing next to me swiveled his head as if looking for a literal phantom reason for my question. "So you're adding a ghost to your plan?"

I wasn't the only person in Alfheim with a terrible poker face. Lennart looked as if he was about call Arne and ask his king to take me away. "Frank, you're not making sense," he said.

"Sorry," I answered. "My satchel's ready?" I nodded toward Raven's Gaze. Maybe I could distract him with an enchanted container for Rose's notebook.

The incredulous look didn't fade. "Are you sure you're all right?" He moved his hands through the space around my shoulders and chest as if checking for wounds in my personal magical space.

"I'm fine, Lennart," I said as I walked toward the restaurant.

He clearly did not believe me. He walked at my side, but his magic danced between the two of us.

I'd freaked out a friend because I literally could not tell him a truth I wanted to share. "I saw something over there." I pointed over my shoulder at the church. "And I went to look."

He looked around again. "What did you see?"

Bjorn would have walked away by now. Arne would have changed the subject. Dag would have ignored the entire situation. "A friend," I said.

Lennart blinked as if momentarily confused, and the closing off happened. "Marcus Aurelius?" he asked.

But not a complete closing off. "What do you think happened to him?" I asked.

Lennart thought for a second. His stormy magic reached upward as if asking the sky a question, then settled onto his being. He grinned and squeezed my shoulder. "Your dog is fine." He thought for a second. "He's a special hound who will help us all one day."

This was the closest I'd gotten an elf to talking about Ellie. It wasn't much, but it felt important.

Lennart nodded knowingly, then leaned toward me. "Bjorn would be inconsolable if one of his cats ran away."

I had a sudden flash of the bear-like thunder elf Bjorn Thorsson filling the entire town with rolling waves of magic as he searched under every porch and in every bush for one of his fifteen-pound balls of fluff.

If I could send out magic like that to overcome Ellie's enchantments, I would.

"Yeah," I said.

We stood together for a moment under the warm afternoon sun, two large men who weren't always at their best among people but who fully understood the magic of an animal companion.

Lennart smiled. "Come! I have someone you should meet." He pulled me toward Raven's Gaze.

Now that the nights were getting colder, the staff of the restaurant had put away about half the normal outdoor seating, and only five tables framed the entrance. The loud kids from the parking lot had spread out around three, and were laughing and leaning against each other as they thumbed through screens on their phones.

We moved toward the break between the buildings and the end-of-season vegetables in the huge gardens, toward the loft at the back of the brewery where Bjorn and Lennart lived.

Lennart, still smiling, stopped under one of the big red oak trees in front of the brewery and pointed up at the branches. "Take a look."

Two ravens sat in the tree. They were bigger than most of the ravens that nested around the lakes, and seemed to be less annoyed by humans than most other corvids.

The smaller of the two watched me from its sheltered spot inside the rustling, leathery, autumn leaves of the giant oak. It bopped a few times and trilled in my general direction.

The larger one clucked as if reprimanding its partner for paying attention to a person.

"Are you two Huginn and Muninn?" Perhaps Bjorn had brought

them in for ambiance. Or perhaps they were scouts. When I was in Las Vegas, I had suggested to the World Raven that she should come by and check out the brewery.

Both birds honked, and the bigger one hopped down a branch to get a better look at me. I held out my arm. Why, I didn't know. It just seemed the correct thing to do.

The big one swooped down and landed on my bicep, then hopped up to my shoulder.

"Well, hello," I said. Magic danced across his plumage, and when he shook, greens, blues, and purples rose like sparks before settling again onto his feathers.

He clucked, then whistled a little tune, and the smaller one dropped down to the lowest branch to watch.

Raven's Gaze Brewery and Pub had its own pair of magical ravens.

"Did Raven send you?" I asked.

Lennart held out his arm and the big raven flapped over to his bracer. "I've been wondering that myself," he said.

His magic snapped and sparked like a summer storm complete with eddies and clouds. He controlled it, though, and channeled it into strong, sturdy spells that might not be delicate, but which stood against most everything.

"They showed up a few days ago," Lennart said. "This is Ross." Lennart stroked the raven's head. "He's friendlier than Betsy up there." He nodded toward the smaller raven still in the tree.

Betsy and Ross. I chuckled. "Their magic looks like a dusting on their feathers," I said.

Lennart clucked at Ross and moved his arm so that the big bird would return to the tree. Then he whistled, and Betsy flew down.

The birds liked him, obviously, so I doubted we were looking at dark magic.

He rubbed Betsy's head. "The names are temporary, aren't they, darling?"

Betsy clucked.

"I'll figure out who you really are soon enough." Lennart kissed the raven, then shooed her back to the tree. "The mundanes have realized we have two new employees." He nodded to the birds. "Bjorn expects a news crew from The Cities to show up before Samhain." He frowned. "He likes the idea. For the publicity." Lennart did not want mundanes with cameras hanging around. "How was the re-wedding?" he asked.

I still looked like a groomsman, even with the hole in my pants. "Arne and Dag got a bouncy castle for the kids," I said.

Lennart laughed. "I take it you did not have time to romp inside the inflated vinyl balloon of doom."

"No," I said. Not that I would have.

He watched the ravens groom each other up in the branches. "Every child in Alfheim loves you," he said offhandedly.

Lennart often uttered random sentences, but "every child" loving me seemed... odd.

"Akeyla have fun?" he asked.

"Other than that photographer interrupting, I think so." He'd shown up here, too. "He was over by the church, by the way. The photographer." I wanted to tell Lennart about Ellie hiding me, and the man's attitude, but once again, not much would come out. "I saw his shadow again." I hadn't, but it got the idea across. "He's carrying a hidden magic of some kind."

Lennart's eyes narrowed. "He got away from you?" He peered up at my face as if looking for signs of a magical infestation. "Is that why you were talking about ghosts?" He stepped back and tapped his fingers on his thigh.

A sigil formed. "There was magic, alright, even if you couldn't see it," he said.

Lennart was making several assumptions about what happened. Some were wrong, some were close enough, and they did get him to the correct place. "Raven's Gaze has security cameras, correct?"

"Of course."

"He didn't do anything other than be annoying," I said. "He's shown up twice and been a thorn. No overt bad behavior." What were we supposed to do? We had an obnoxious visitor with shadowy magic.

Alfheim had what Ed would call a "person of interest" who hadn't done anything bad but exasperated law enforcement anyway.

Lennart thought for a moment. His eyes narrowed again. "I'll check the church when we're done." He turned back toward the loft, and his body subtly stiffened and he changed the subject. "Did Maura enjoy the wedding?" He continued to look away.

I had no idea he held an interest in Maura. "She and all the bridesmaids were as lovely as you would expect," I said.

He rubbed at the back of his Bulldogs cap. "Good, good," he said.

His attraction to Maura danced through his magic and screamed out to the world as loudly as any exhibited by the teenagers jabbering at the tables behind us. "We all missed you at the wedding," I said.

He patted his ear to remind me that glamouring around mundanes wasn't easy for him. Then he grinned and nodded toward the brewery building. "Come. I've taken good care of Rose's notebook for you." With that, he walked toward the loft behind the buildings.

I looked up at Betsy and Ross. "Tell Raven if she wants to get a burger, I'll make reservations." I pointed at the eatery.

Betsy bobbed her head. Ross fluttered his wings and groomed his tail. Then they both flew higher into the tree.

Magical or not, they were still ravens. I grinned and followed Lennart.

He pushed open the wide door leading into the living quarters and ushered me inside. The UMD hat sailed toward a side table and coat rack just to our left, and the door banged shut behind us.

Lennart dropped all pretense of glamouring. His tall ears fully manifested, as did the intricate, coiling tattoos covering his neck, jaw, and the naked curve of his scalp.

Magic formed storm clouds around his body, and for a second, I wondered if it would condense out as rain. It didn't, though, but kept with its roiling and boiling, as one would expect from a thunder god's aspect.

Bjorn's magic wasn't nearly as chaotic as Lennart's. Bjorn had a calmness to him one would not normally attribute to Thor. His magic drew people in, patted them on the back, and offered them revelry and entertainment.

The loft mirrored their dichotomy. The ageless tension between clutter and cleanliness fought each other like warriors of Valhalla, from the spotless desk in one corner to the couch covered in a raucous heap of distinctly patterned, handmade throws. Almost every surface had at least one potted plant. Sun streamed in from the high windows. A woodsy scent, complete with the higher humidity that came with so much foliage, hung evenly in the air.

The loft was a modern elf's paradise.

Summer Sassafras—one of Bjorn's queen Norwegian Forest cats—sashayed out of the sunroom and right up to my ankles. She meowed and rubbed, but batted away my hand when I tried to pet her fluffy grey and white head.

"Is Mr. Mole Rat bothering you again?" Lennart picked her up and scratched her neck. "I keep telling Bjorn we need to get that cat fixed or one of the ladies will do it for us."

Mr. Mole Rat padded out of the sunroom looking more pleased with himself than he probably had a right to be.

Sass hissed. Lennart set her down. "Sass here has no time for Cranky Rat, do you?"

She meowed, hissed at Mr. Mole Rat once again, and sashayed away toward her normal nap zone.

"She hates him," Lennart said. "The only thing keeping him from dismemberment is magic."

For elves who prided themselves on the quality of their kittens, having a disruptive tom around seemed counterproductive. "Why does Bjorn keep him?"

Lennart shrugged. "Benta."

During an off period in my on-and-off-again relationship with Benta, she'd taken up briefly with Bjorn.

I shook my head and vowed not to allow our final break-up to turn petty. One would expect better from elves, but I've lived with them for two hundred years and knew better.

Mr. Mole Rat let out a "Why are you here?" yowl. Then he flopped down in the middle of the cat bed next to the desk.

"Benta and I are done," I said. We'd talked and formally ended all romantic entanglements after I returned from Las Vegas.

Lennart sniffed as if he only partly believed me, but smiled. His magic settled. "Come! The satchel's in here." He walked toward the sun room.

Summer Sassafras napped as a ball of cat on top of one of the sunnier cat condos. Her sister, the almost-black tabby Winter Watermelon, raised her head from the top of her condo inside a gated-off section of the room. She let out a meow-yawn as Lennart walked by.

Five big, fluffy kittens bounced up to the gate. A chorus of meows and purrs followed.

Lennart scooped one up. "It's time to find you a new home, huh?"

The kitten purred and rubbed against Lennart's sideburn.

"Akeyla wants one," I said.

Lennart blinked as if I'd just offered him the moon. "Bring her by! She'll have the pick of the litter, huh, sweetie?" The kitten headbutted his hand and let out a solid purr.

He smiled again, set the kitten back behind the gate, and then rummaged around on the wide worktable taking up most of the sunroom's space. "Ah!" He held up a lovely leather satchel that he'd hand-tooled with runic sigils.

A tight bubble of stasis magic very much like the one surrounding Remy's pouches sheathed the satchel. "Is it the same suspension spell as Remy's?" I asked.

He held out the bag. "Your ability to see magic is a precious gift, Frank Victorsson." He grinned. "Took some research to find the spell, by the way."

I took the bag. "Thank you for this," I said.

He shrugged. "No matter how our King and Queen dislike the witch's book, it has a purpose. And value. You are correct to protect it."

Out in the main living area, the door roared open. "I'm home!" thundered Bjorn.

Lennart's magic... re-adjusted. It didn't calm, or change, but seemed to re-orient as if pushed by a new air current. He patted my arm. "Say hello to Maura and Akeyla for us."

Bjorn strode into the sunroom, looked around, and placed his hands on his hips. "All set?" he asked.

I held up the satchel.

"Good. Good!" He tossed his suit jacket at one of the cat condos. "Remy Geroux is checking in Las Vegas to make sure the Wolf encountered there isn't behind our new friend's intrusion."

"Good," I said. *Not* adding a kitten to my bundle as I walked by turned out to be harder than I expected, especially with all the meowing and purring.

Bjorn winked at Lennart as if all of this had been a conspiracy to get me to take one home.

"I'm not sure how my hound would react to a kitten," I said.

Bjorn frowned. "We will find your dog, Frank." He slapped my shoulder. "I'm supposed to ask you to pick up dinner while you're here. Maura said the kids would like burgers."

Jax must be at my place. "Will do." I threw the satchel's strap over my shoulder. "Maybe we should check in at the restaurant to see if he came in there, too," I said to Lennart.

"Why?" Bjorn asked. He touched the tip of his nose, then pointed at me. "Those two ravens weren't giving you trouble, were they?"

"The ravens were friendly," I said.

Lennart tossed a quick look of annoyance at Bjorn. Betsy and Ross were obviously playing favorites between the two Thor elves. "That photographer from the wedding showed up at the church. He was here just long enough to annoy Frank, then he disappeared again."

Bjorn's magic flared. "We do not need distractions this close to a wolf run on Samhain!" he bellowed.

Lennart's magic responded with its own roiling flare. He closed his eyes and pinched his lips as if the moment caused him pain. "Bjorn," he said, "do you have that memory card?"

Bjorn's magic instantly settled. Lennart's followed. Bjorn squeezed the other elf's shoulder. "Yes, yes," he said, then waved to me. "I'll call when we find something," he called.

I gave Bjorn a thumbs-up as I walked toward the door. I looked over my shoulder just as the elves dropped into a deep discussion about concealment enchantments and what spells they could try to unmask the magic underneath.

I left them to their magicks, somehow making it out of the loft without a kitten, and pulled out my phone to text Maura halfway to the eatery's front door.

CHAPTER 7

T he guitar riffs and steady cadence of blues rhythms boomed
from Raven's Gaze. Bjorn and Lennart might be metal, but
blues sold more hamburgers, and the manager on duty had particularly good musical taste.

I walked back toward the restaurant after putting the satchel in my
truck. No need to carry it and chance a tourist asking where I got it.

I realized I still needed to text Maura and find out what kind of
burgers the kids wanted. My surprise when I opened my phone and
looked down at the photo of my mystery woman—Ellie, goddamn it
—got me every time I swiped my phone's screen. Every. Single.
Time.

An entire encyclopedia's worth of colorful language rolled from
my throat as I walked under the rustling leaves of the red oak. Only
one of the ravens hopped among the branches. It cawed, bobbed its
head at my language, and disappeared into the leaves at the oak's
crown.

I didn't dare jokingly ask the ravens for help. The last thing I
needed was a bored world spirit trickster poking at my concealment
enchantment mess.

Inside the restaurant, the manager—a nondescript mundane from town with a mop of brown hair and a thinner build than most of the locals—nodded once and went back to his cleaning duties.

I sat next to the Halloween jack-o-lantern decoration on the end of the bar and held up my phone so he could look at the photo of Ellie with my dog. "Do you recognize this woman?" I asked.

He frowned. "No," he answered. "Is she a tourist?"

So she hadn't come in, either before or after she ran away. My notes said mundanes tended to remember her until nightfall.

I shook my head. "I have her bicycle," I said.

"Ah," he said. "If she comes in, I'll let her know."

"Thanks," I said.

I thumbed through my phone plan while I waited for the takeout. Turned out I already had two lines. One had been used briefly around the time Dracula pulled me into Vampland, then nothing.

It must be the phone Ellie lost. I put in an order for a new phone and a reactivation of the number at our local store. If I was fast, I could pick it up before dinner got too cold.

The stool next to mine squeaked.

My peripheral vision isn't as good as an elf's. It's probably a little worse overall than the average mundane's—another of my father's many "gifts"—but I've had two centuries to teach my brain to compensate. Like everything else about my piecemeal body, I've put in the work needed to maximize what I did have.

Or so I thought.

The small photographer in the expensive suit leaned against the bar as if he'd been there for minutes and was annoyed that I'd just now noticed him.

He scrunched up his nose and loudly inhaled. "Mr. Victorsson," he said.

"Who are you?" I demanded more than asked. I was beginning to think he wasn't the semi-local photographer he claimed.

He did the loud inhale again as if Raven's Gaze, and me in particular, offended his olfactory senses. "How is it that elves can be so disorganized? It's like a slow-motion Ragnarok around here."

This man was a liar who knew about Alfheim's magicals.

In the restaurant's pools of halogen lighting I couldn't tell if he carried the shadow, and the backlight from the bar was too diffuse for me to get a good look. "Then you need to take that up with our King and Queen." He wouldn't, of course. Such confrontations were the last thing a sneaky slimeball wanted.

He looked out at the handful of patrons scattered around the seating area. "I've been debating when I should properly introduce myself." He looked me up and down. "There was a shift here recently." He waved his hand at the greater universe. "A change in the air, so to speak; hence the reconnaissance."

He could be referring to the reset the elves unleashed when my brother invaded town. Or he could mean the changes that came after the International Conclave in Las Vegas. Or he could be referring to the more mundane changes in town caused by several shifting economic factors.

Or he could be bloviating.

"What do you want?" Villains liked to talk. Perhaps he'd tell me just to see if I'd squirm.

"A voice, Mr. Victorsson," he said. "A chance to offer Alfheim and her people clear, disciplined, *better* management."

Was this little man threatening Arne and Dagrun?

He laughed. "Who runs a tighter ship, Mr. Victorsson? Elves? Vampires? The fae?" He leaned closer. "Wolves?"

The bar manager stepped up. "Would you like to order?" he asked the man.

Our interloper tapped his pointer fingers together as if trying to stop himself from steepling his hands. "I'll try the local brew," he said.

The manager nodded toward me. "Your order's up." He pointed to the end of the bar.

"Thank you," I said.

The manager nodded again and went off to fetch a pour for the interloper, who pulled a tooled leather wallet from his jacket pocket.

He set a one hundred dollar bill on the bar. "You asked what I wanted," he said.

I did not speak. I waited for an answer.

He looked out over the patrons again. "I want the same as you, Mr. Victorsson. I want solutions to the problems that vex me." The manager returned and set the photographer's glass on the bar. "Thank you," the man said.

The manager stared at the hundred on the counter. "Would you like change for this?" he asked.

The interloper winked. "Pay for Mr. Victorsson's meal, too, please."

"No," I said, forcefully enough that the manager startled a bit. "I will pay for my own food." One should never accept gifts from unknown magicals for any reason or at any time. What if this man was a fae? I'd been stupid enough to make deals with kitsune. I wasn't stupid enough to stumble into a tit-for-tat with a fae, especially since that food would be going home to be eaten by Akeyla and Jax.

But my gut said I wasn't dealing with a fae. My gut said he was something closer to home.

I handed the manager my credit card. He nodded, and walked toward the register.

"I see you lack the courtesy to accept a simple gesture of good will," the interloper said into his beer. "Mmmm... this is excellent."

No more veiled threats from the little mobster sitting next to me. I pulled out my phone. *I need you at the bar*, I texted Bjorn. *He's here.*

"Now, now." He sipped his beer again, then set it on the bar. "I do not take kindly to threats."

He knew about the magicals in town, yet showed no obvious magic himself. He dressed like a rich man who hadn't been rich long enough to grow any sense, much less taste. And he talked as if he was Loki himself. "What do you *want?*" I asked again, because this man was trouble. I just couldn't tell for sure if he was the dark trouble the wolves sensed this morning.

Yet there was no doubt I was sitting next to the source of shadow. Maybe not of the spell itself, but at least its machinations.

"Solace, Mr. Victorsson." He sipped again. "A righting of wrongs. An end to my vexations."

Bjorn's magic burst through the door before he did, and rolled out like a green- and violet-infused storm.

The interloper slapped the bar. He downed his remaining beer, and turned toward the big elf striding toward us. "Stay back!" He held up his hands.

Bjorn didn't break stride. "Who the hell are you?" he semi-shouted. He held up his phone. "The photographer you claimed to be is six-foot-three and sixty-two years old."

The interloper held up his hands. "I will know if you lay one ounce of your elven glory upon my person," he said.

"Get out of my pub," Bjorn growled.

"I paid Mr. Wilson a lot of money to rent his equipment," the little man said. "And you damaged his camera. I wouldn't be surprised if he sues."

As Bjorn raised his hands to hit the man with some type of magic, the interloper raised his arms as if cowering from a punch.

"You hit me in any way and I will consider it assault!" he yelled. "I will sue you! This restaurant, the brewery, the property next door will be *mine* before any of you can lay down a curse!"

Bjorn stopped. He was obviously as confused as I was. "If you have brought an unwelcome… energy… to our town, I will deal with you personally," he growled.

The manager and the other patrons were watching us, and Bjorn had dialed back any talk of magic.

The interloper grinned. He smoothed his jacket and resettled his gold chain. And he sniffed loudly once again. "It wounds me to see how uncivilized and insular this little community is." He rolled his shoulders. "The shame it must bring."

Bjorn threw me a *what is he talking about?* look. I shrugged.

The interloper made a show of flashing his gold pinky ring as he adjusted his cufflinks. "Move to the side. I wish to pass."

Bjorn growled loudly enough to startle the manager even though he was at the other end of the bar.

The entire restaurant was quiet. Only the beat of the blues music and the slight rattle from the kitchen filled the air.

No magic danced. Bjorn kept his thunder and lightning back.

The interloper walked right up to him. Bjorn stared down at the little man and refused to move.

They stood like that—too close and exuding dominance—until the interloper laughed. He touched the tip of his nose and threw out his arms as if to hug Bjorn.

The big elf very quickly moved out of reach.

The interloper sneered. He winked at the manager and bowed to the other patrons, then blew Bjorn a kiss.

Bjorn grabbed for him, but I caught his arm. "Careful," I said.

The interloper strutted toward the exit, but stopped and placed his back against the glass. "Good meeting!" he shouted, then backed out of the restaurant.

The backlighting from the afternoon sun should have shadowed his face. His expression should have been difficult to read. It was not. He smirked like a child who had just stolen candy and knew he was going to get away with it.

But mostly, what should have been shadowed was not, and what should have been bright was shadowed. He might not have obvious magic, but something around him caused a distortion. He saluted, then sauntered outside.

Bjorn took a step toward the door.

"Stay here," I said. The last thing we needed was a full-on magic fight in the parking lot within the view of mundanes. I grabbed my phone and pushed through the exit into the bright afternoon sun— and onto an empty patio. No patrons. No interloper.

He'd vanished. I jogged out to the scattered vehicles in the lot, none of which were making a getaway. Had he returned to the church? I peered at the trees and the building. Nothing moved, but I made my way over anyway.

I swiped open my phone as I jogged. *He's gone*, I texted Bjorn. *Call Ed and pull the security footage.* He'd call Arne on his own, and the wolves. *I'm checking the church.* He didn't have many other options other than around back, but Lennart was still at the back of the pub and brewery, and I doubt he would have gone toward an elf.

I rounded the corner onto the path leading to the church and...

stopped. Betsy, the smaller of the two ravens, perched on a small, leather rectangle in the middle of the walk. The church loomed directly behind her and in perfect alignment. She held her neck and back at a forty-five-degree angle to the church's corner column. The saint I'd almost punched sat up and over her tail, while the carved Yggdrasil-like tree of the church's door framed her head.

I knew what I was looking at. I understood. Geometry was one of the ways the mundane world accessed otherwise inaccessible magic.

Except these two birds were not mundane. Not at all.

"Did you see where he went?" I asked.

Betsy preened her chest. With each feather cleaned, magic puffed off her as little crackling clouds of blue-silver energy. I squatted down.

She squawked instead, and flew off when I extended my arm hoping she'd hop up for a talk.

"You two aren't exactly clear with your thoughts and memories!" I shouted. Off in the trees, the two ravens laughed.

I picked up the leather rectangle. The package was about the size of a postcard, more of a sleeve than an envelope or pouch, and contained a plate of some sort.

I carefully held it up and scanned it for any unwanted spells, then gently tugged the plate from the sleeve—and uncovered a daguerreo-type photograph. A richly colored one, with hues beyond the sepia tones the copper and silver of the process allowed. Hues that lifted off the plate as if I was looking more at a hologram than a photo.

My lake shimmered gently in the photo's background, along with the Carlsons' in-process house. Soft, natural magic lifted from the water, and the remnants of my brother's ash magic from the Carlson place.

The photo picked up subtle magicks that I often did not notice.

In the photo, I sat on the mat on my deck in my shorts, shirtless to maximize my skin's exposure to the sun, looking up at the morning sky. Faint magic twisted around me in balanced, concentric circles as if I'd drawn the natural magic of my world into the residual elven magic I always seemed to carry.

Nothing looked out of place. Nothing about my world was out-of-whack.

Ellie, I thought. How I knew she'd taken the photo and not our interloper, I couldn't say consciously, but my gut knew. So did my heart, and my soul. She'd caught me at a moment of peace.

She wanted me to see myself balanced.

And she was telling me I would be fine without her.

My breath hitched. "No, I will not," I said. The photo didn't show the concealment enchantments infecting her life and the lives of everyone in Alfheim. The same enchantments that kept that faint magic from becoming fully realized.

"I'm not giving up," I said. I looked at the parking lot in case she was still nearby. "I'm not, Ellie!" I yelled. Then out into the trees. "I won't!"

From the Raven's Gaze side of the trees, I got my answer. *Wonk wonk!* one of the ravens yelled. *Caw!* the other answered.

The desire to punch the church returned. To do so would not help. I'd end up with a sore wrist along with my ripped-up heart.

And this time, I did curse the magic. I cursed and I stomped, and gripped the photo.

"Frank!" Bjorn yelled from the Raven's Gaze side of the trees.

Another elf come to interrupt an Ellie moment. This time, though, I was thankful. "I'm not," I muttered again.

Perhaps a distraction would allow me to parse what all this meant. Or perhaps not. I tucked the photo back into its sleeve, righted myself. What else was I to do? We had an interloper to hunt.

CHAPTER 8

By the time I got home the sun had dropped to just above the trees and cast a warm glow over my driveway. The road side of my house had sunk fully into shadow when I parked, but the motion sensors on the string lights between the house and Maura's wine-bottle gate flickered on as I turned off my truck.

Fall crispness chilled the air. My breath formed an icy cloud as I walked around to the passenger side to retrieve the evening's gatherings.

Raven's Gaze had been a flurry of magical activity by the time I walked back over after finding Ellie's photo. Bjorn had already called Arne and Dag, and was on the phone with Gerard when I entered. Security footage was pulled shortly thereafter, then Ed called.

I dropped Ellie's photo into the satchel, settled the strap onto my shoulder, picked up the takeout and the new phone, and came home. Anyone who wanted my story could call tomorrow.

How was I supposed to respond to Ellie not wanting me to find a way inside her enchantments when she clearly wanted—needed—me to? I hadn't yet lost today's encounter to the memory pit of the concealments.

She said *I miss you so much.*

She missed me. She kissed me. But I'm not supposed to make sure she's okay?

Sal *humphed*.

"What?" I asked. A steady stream of mild irritation had been washing off her since we left Raven's Gaze.

I pulled her out of her pocket and set her on the seat next to the food and the phone while I placed the satchel's strap over my shoulder.

The bag swung over her blade.

Sal shot me a stern *please keep that away from me*.

"Why?" I asked. They were both elf magic, and therefore compatible.

Compatible, yes, but the stasis enchantments interfered with her ability to watch the world.

"Noted." I tucked my jacket over the satchel, swung Sal onto my opposite shoulder, and picked up the packages. "We'll need to figure out where to store Rose's notebook so the spells don't give you a headache." I walked toward the house.

She thanked me.

"You're welcome, my friend—"

An angry Akeyla-made screech rose from the other side of the house, and a bright flare of fire magic shot into the air from my deck and crested the roof.

Something—or someone—had pissed off my niece.

I rounded the side of the house at the same time Maura slammed the screen door leading from the house to the deck.

"What's wrong?" She moved to the kids before I set the packages on the table near the door.

Maura usually didn't glamour at home, so her calm, ice-like magic flowed gently around her body. It reached down the deck, toward the kids.

Akeyla and Jax stood at the end of the deck by the lake, both more comfortably dressed than they had been for the wedding, scowling at each other. Jax crossed his arms and looked up at the moon. Akeyla pressed her fists into her hips.

"I'll do my schoolwork the way I want!" she yelled.

Maura squatted so she'd be on the same level with the kids. "What are you two fighting about?"

Akeyla leaned toward Jax, but didn't take her fists off her hips. "He says I need to stop doing my homework because Ms. Saunders said I can skip a grade and we need to finish high school at the same time or he won't get a schol... scholar..."

"Scholarship," Jax said. He still wouldn't look at Akeyla.

"A scholarship to the University to play baseball and I'm his mate so it's my job to make sure he can play and I have to run with him when he's at away games no matter what so I can't go to college first."

Maura looked up at me as if to ask *Did you get any of that?*

I set Sal against the deck railing. "Neither of you will be applying for scholarships until you're seniors," I said. Not that either of them would need scholarships to pay for school. Having an immortal family helps a lot with wealth accumulation.

Jax rolled his eyes. "We *know.*"

"Then what's the problem?" I asked.

"He wants me to act dumb so Ms. Saunders will tell the fourth-grade teachers to keep me in the same class with him." Akeyla's magic flared again.

"That's not a nice thing to ask someone to do, Jax," Maura said.

Jax's scowl deepened. "But I'm alpha and she's my mate."

Akeyla shoved Jax. "They're *your* games! Not *mine!*"

"Hey, hey, honey." Maura pulled Akeyla away from Jax. "Let's all go in and eat dinner." She pointed at the takeout on the table. "We'll talk about this calmly."

If anything, Maura's suggestion made Jax dig in his heels even more. And being the young alpha that he was, nothing about his body relaxed. He continued to square his shoulders to the women and stand with his feet apart and his arms crossed over his chest.

Dominance posture on a nine-year-old werewolf isn't cute. If anything, it's frightening, because a nine-year-old doesn't understand what he's doing. An angry nine-year-old, even a born wolf—even Jax

—was only marginally better at controlling his wolf than the newly turned.

And one-on-one, not much was more dangerous than a raging werewolf.

"Perhaps you need to go home and think about what you said to Akeyla," Maura said. "Whether or not she skips a grade is up to her, not you. Apologize."

Jax snorted.

Tears burst from Akeyla. She wailed and hugged her mother. "I don't like him anymore," she said against her mother's shoulder.

Jax's magic growled. *He* didn't, thank goodness, but his wolf looked at Maura, then me, and released an angry vibration.

"Jaxson!" Maura snapped.

"You are hurting Akeyla. Stop," I said. Jaxson Geroux was firmly entrenched inside his little nine-year-old alpha ditch and utterly unable to see that his hole wasn't a hill.

Jaxson looked away. Maura's eyes widened for a split second, and Akeyla continued to bury her face in her mother's shoulder.

Maura stood and pulled Akeyla to her hip. "You're going home, young man. Your behavior is unacceptable." She turned Akeyla toward the door.

My little fire elf niece ran up the deck to the door sniffling and trailing a bright tail of blue and red magic.

Maura stopped next to the table and glanced at me. I nodded, and she picked up dinner and the other items, then followed her daughter inside.

Jax continued to frown, but had turned away and stared up at the moon. His wolf magic shimmered in the moonglow as a silver-violet bubble with paws and a snout.

Hierarchy and dominance didn't blend well with the whole fated-mate business. The hierarchy part of the package wasn't canine. I'd lived too long with dogs and the Alfheim Pack to have any doubts about what was wolf and what was human.

I walked to the edge of the deck, stopped, and consciously mimicked Jax's alpha stance.

He looked me up and down, and returned to staring at the moon.

"You may have already chosen her, but that doesn't mean she will choose you when the time comes," I said.

He frowned. "We're fated."

I rubbed my cheek. "No," I said. "You're compatible. You're friends." I waved at the house. "Or you used to be friends. You've got some hefty repair work ahead of you."

He glanced at the house and somehow managed to deepen his already subterranean frown.

Jax was a good kid with a good head on his shoulders, and generally mature for his nine years. But it was clear that his cooperation was never because of social pressure. He cooperated because he believed it was the best way to secure the pack.

And in his head, "securing the pack" meant maintaining his alphaness at peak efficiency. Everyone in the pack must agree. If they didn't, they weren't pack. Nor was he alpha.

He was having trouble seeing around his circular young-man thinking.

"What did you think of the wedding today?" I asked. I wasn't the most qualified to talk to anyone about mates and marriage. My past with women was complicated. But I was outside the pack and elf hierarchy, so perhaps I could offer guidance that Jax might otherwise ignore.

He rubbed his cheek as if mimicking me. "We're both going to college," he said, as if he'd rehearsed this moment many times and wanted to cut through the small talk. Or perhaps he'd already had a similar talk with his father and uncle. "If Akeyla skips a year we won't graduate at the same time."

"This worries you?"

He looked up at me the same way Akeyla looked up at her dumb Uncle Frank.

I held back a sigh. "Her schooling is hers. What she does is not your decision." Not now. Not in the future, either. "She will ask for your opinion, Jax. If you are fated, she will treasure your advice and your help. That's not the same thing as you telling her what to do."

And what about me? Ellie had pretty much told me to stop my attempts to find my way inside her enchantments. I would fix her bike. I'd picked up her new phone. But I wasn't to do anything more.

I frowned as much as Jax did.

He shrugged. Was I surprised by his bullheadedness? He was a Geroux, and a proto-alpha. But he was in for a rude awakening if he thought everyone needed to bow to his wishes.

"So you two have already planned your graduations?" Of course they had, but in a third grade, best friends way.

"If Akeyla comes with me, I can play out-of-state games."

And if I find a way into Ellie's enchantments, I could help her find a way out.

Or so I believed.

"Well, yes," I said. "Maybe. It won't be that simple." How much was Akeyla willing to sacrifice for Jax? What was he asking her to do? I looked out over the lake, at the moon streaking across the water and the faster-than-expected rebuilding of the Carlson house.

Helping Ellie wasn't that simple, either. Every evening, I went out looking for a woman I felt compelled to help. A woman who meant more to me than I remembered and who wanted me to stop.

"Friendships are complicated," I said. Friendships and relationships.

Over against the fence, Sal huffed.

Jax looked at the axe. "What's her problem?"

Sal found the little wolf's attitude wanting. His alpha-ness was moot when it came to elves.

I chuckled. Of course Sal would only consider the elf part of this problem. "She also thinks you need to apologize to Akeyla," I said.

Jax sighed and dropped his arms to his sides, but didn't respond.

"I'm going to be straight with you," I said. Maybe I needed to learn the same lesson. "I'm not going to talk down to you, son." I wasn't going to squat the way Maura did, though. Playing the physical hierarchy might get him to listen.

He nodded.

"When your mom went to college, what happened?" He needed to learn that no one's ditch was isolated from the other ditches in the community.

"Dad drove to Fargo every full moon," he said.

The deliberations around Axlam's college years had been a major event in Alfheim. The pack had long wanted to increase their integration into mundane life, and to test living away from the central group. Axlam was the first candidate who had the will, creativity, and intelligence to try it.

The wolves and the elves made a plan and set up a schedule. Axlam made it through four years at the University of North Dakota in Fargo with zero mishaps. She graduated with honors, and came home with the training necessary to help Dag manage the city—and a mate.

"Or your mother drove home. That was not a small feat for either of them, or for the pack." Axlam had come home from Fargo about the same time Maura had gone to Hawaii. "An elf always went with your father when your mother couldn't come home."

She'd had full buy-in. She'd had community help, and a mate capable of communicating with her about every aspect of the journey.

"Jax," I said, "the point is that you will be asking a lot more of Akeyla than either of you realize right now."

Was I asking more of Ellie than I realized? I forgot her every evening. I'd be forgetting her within the next half-hour for sure, once the sun fully descended behind the horizon.

And every morning, I yelled out for her anew. I wailed like a little kid who didn't understand why my best friend had moved away.

"I know," he said. "We're kids and we don't understand adult things." His wolf reared up. "It's not like we're going to have a baby!" His innate wolf magic flared.

Babies, I thought. A possible family.

I set aside the thought and stared down his flaring magic. "I'm going to leave explaining *that* bit of your mate magic to your parents," I said.

His wolf subsided, but this time, he did roll his eyes.

"My point," I said, "is that one day you will be the alpha of your aspirations. And if you value yourself more than you do her, fated mate or not, you will lose your best friend."

Was I even capable of carrying my own burden? How could I possibly understand Ellie's if I didn't understand my own?

He blinked and his face contorted with kid confusion. His body tensed and his wolf magic reformed.

It snarled, not at me, but at the wider world—as if anger was creeping in to replace his inability to grasp what I said.

And I wondered if, once the concealments wiped my memory tonight, all I'd have left was my own creeping rage.

I would never allow that rage near Ellie. Had I already? Was that why she told me to go away?

Jax didn't understand, but I sure understood allowing rage to kick away any sense of an overwhelming world. Rage was much easier to understand than other people's needs. Rage always elicited fear, and other people's fear was familiar. Other people's fear I could control.

"Akeyla is mine," he whispered.

Not good, I thought. "No," I said.

He—and his wolf—frowned again.

"I know it feels like she is yours." I needed to make this more concrete, or he'd get lost in his anger. "If Akeyla is going to skip a grade, she has to work extra hard and prove to her teacher that she can handle fifth grade next year, right?"

He nodded.

"Why would she do that?" I asked.

He stared at the Carlson house, but his wolf settled down into a contemplative shadow. "Because she likes school."

"Yes," I said. "You're excellent at baseball, and good at school. Akeyla is excellent at school and good at baseball. You have common interests, but different preferences."

He groaned. "She's not good at baseball, Mr. Frank."

I shrugged. "She could be, if she wanted to. She's an elf."

The frown returned.

"Jax, you demanded that Akeyla exchange her preferences for yours. How would you feel if she did that to you?"

His attention suddenly, utterly shifted away from me. He perked up and craned his neck to look around the house. "Mom and Dad are here."

He wasn't going to answer. Not with the distraction of his parents' arrival. Hopefully he wouldn't forget any of our exchange—the way I'd be forgetting about my moment with Ellie at the church. I'd forget, and not learn my lesson.

I counted three, two, one... and the faint glow of headlights swept the house. Axlam and Gerard pulled into the driveway.

"Do you understand what I mean?" I patted Jax's shoulder. "You need to be more than a good friend, Jaxson. You need to be Akeyla's *best* friend. Always."

I still wasn't sure he understood, but he and his wolf had calmed. At least he seemed to be contemplating what I said.

"Make sure you say good-bye to Akeyla and her mom," I called. "Don't forget your burger."

He looked over his shoulder. "Thank you, Mr. Frank." He ran toward the door.

I'd need to have a talk with Gerard and Axlam about our conversation. Maura, too. Hopefully I'd helped.

Sal reminded me that I'd left her leaning against the deck rail.

"Yes?" I asked.

She wanted to know if I was going to keep my promise to take her for a walk tonight.

"A walk?" I asked. I usually went out at night for an hour or two looking for Ellie.

She was out there, somewhere. Alone, and I hoped okay. I didn't know, or at least I didn't think I knew. I'd been keeping notes on my phone. I should probably check them before going to bed tonight.

I watched Gerard squat down so he was at his son's height. He placed his hand on Jax's shoulder. Words were spoken. Jax looked at the floor.

Slowly and self-consciously, Jax walked over to the table, where Akeyla ate her burger. He touched her arm.

She pulled away and wouldn't look at him.

Jax slumped. His face fell. And the consequences of his behavior landed fully on his young soul.

He looked up at his father, who shook his head. Jax picked up his meal from the stack and walked away, presumably toward his parents' car.

Akeyla chewed. Gerard followed his son toward the door, with Axlam and Maura following behind. And I stood on the deck watching everyone leave my little niece to eat her fries alone.

Something that, at least tonight, she seemed perfectly happy to do.

Sal tossed me another request for walk.

I rubbed my forehead and looked out along the lakeshore. "I should go in," I said. My burger was getting cold, and my family needed me.

Ellie needed me, or so I told myself every night when I walked into the woods to search for stray magic and my dog.

Or maybe she didn't. Maybe I needed her. Maybe I was intruding into a life I had no business touching.

Women were confusing.

I swung Sal onto my shoulder. "Maybe later," I said, and walked away from the woods and toward the bright, burger-scented kitchen.

CHAPTER 9

I t turned out our interloper had showed up two more times on Saturday, first at the Wolftown Gallery, and later still at Alfheim's main grocery store out on the highway. Both times he'd sauntered in, done a lot of sniffing, and made a scene. Nothing broken, thank goodness, but he did rant about the "tribal" art at the gallery. And at the grocery store, he complained about the "pedestrian" deli choices.

Then he vanished. No security camera picked up a car with a license to trace. None of the local hotels or resorts had anyone staying who matched his description.

I was beginning to think that Alfheim had been crashed by the world spirit of Entitled Arrogance.

Thing was, the Wolftown Gallery was within three blocks of the homes of half the Alfheim Pack's members, and according to Ed, no one had sensed anything weird. Same for the one elf who'd been in the grocery store.

That was five days ago. He'd left behind no magicks, and had somehow managed to avoid leaving any clear security footage. No one had seen—or sensed—him since.

Not me. Not Ed or any of the elves. Not the pack. Our interloper had disappeared as quickly as he'd appeared.

So Alfheim went about her business of preparing for the Samhain runs and the coming blizzard.

Because we most definitely had a blizzard coming. I felt it in my bones—and on the skin of my face. The morning was the coolest yet, as if the coming storms wanted to make sure all of Alfheim remembered to buy milk and coffee, and to make sure we all had gas for our generators and wood for our fireplaces. I left the garage door open anyway, for the bright Thursday morning light.

I probably should have dug around for a space heater.

Still, I had a bike in my garage that needed fixing. The kids had Thursday and Friday off for the yearly Minnesota Educators conference, and Akeyla was home, so I figured today was a good day to at least get one chore out of the way.

Turned out that the green bike's brakes needed tightening. The rear tire also needed replacing—a patch would hold, but both tires were worn and in bad shape. The frame showed a little rust, too, and at least two coats of paint under the green—one red, and under that a thick layer of orange. The entire crank and pedal assembly wobbled enough that the chain easily slipped off the gears.

The frame had a heft to it that modern bikes did not, and all the mechanisms were well-worn and heavily used.

I wiped my hands on a rag and stepped back. The garage needed cleaning before the snow hit, otherwise Maura's sedan would be out on the gravel with Bloodyhood. I couldn't get the truck into the garage with the plow, so Maura might as well use it.

But for the moment I had an old forest green bike leaning on its loose kickstand in the middle of the garage floor as I tested its parts and wiggled its bits.

"Vintage" best described the bike's workings. It was a lovely bit of craftsmanship, but like all old things that had lived a good life, it really needed to retire.

I pulled out my phone to snap a few images of the frame. Perhaps the shop in town could get me the parts I—

And there she was looking out at me, my sad-eyed mystery woman hugging my wayward dog.

Her name was Ellie. Ellie Jones. I had notes.

The bike was hers.

I looked up at the clear blue of the pre-blizzard sky. I was to fix the bike and leave it with a new cellphone against the outside railing of my deck, near the gap that led to the path into the woods.

That explained why I had a second phone sitting on the kitchen counter next to my landline.

My notes read like a hostage exchange—leave the bike, the phone, your million small, non-sequential doubts and worries under the oak tree or you will never see your dog again.

Why would I be so terse? My healthy and happy hound came home regularly. The hostage here was a woman named Ellie Jones. Or maybe the hostage was me.

I must have talked to her, otherwise I wouldn't have written myself such detailed notes about the bike, or about making sure she had a cellphone.

The bike's handlebars halted and slipped, and I shook my head. "You need to go to the repair shop in town," I said. "I don't have the tools or parts you need here."

I'd take it into town. Ellie couldn't use it until spring, anyway.

I should probably leave the cellphone, though.

The crunching of tires on my gravel drive and the purr of an engine rolled in through the open garage door. I dropped the rag on the table and walked out into the open area between the garage and the house.

Axlam waved as she pulled her sedan around and parked next to Maura's by the front door. She often came by on the weekends with Jax. The kids played while she and Maura had coffee on the deck. But today she was alone.

She fiddled with something on the passenger seat, then unfolded herself from the vehicle.

The wolves were all graceful, but Axlam's grace often matched an elf's, and I'd long suspected her poise would have been there even if she wasn't an alpha werewolf.

Today she wore a silver-blue headscarf that matched her innate magic in both color and shine.

"Sometimes I think you can see magic, too." I circled my finger around my face to indicate the scarf. "You match exquisitely this morning."

She smiled as she walked over. "It seemed the correct color to wear today." She pointed at the sky. "With the storms coming, ya know," she said with her slight Northern Minnesota lilting accent. Axlam mostly sounded as if she lived in The Cities—it helped with City Manager business, she liked to say—but her thirty years in Alfheim did register in her voice.

Up until recently, she'd been the only person of East African descent in the city. There'd been some harassment issues with a few of the outside-of-town locals this past year, but regional Alfheim seemed to be better behaved with our recent immigrants than several other small Minnesota towns.

I was pretty sure the mundane issues wore on her. They wore on Ed, too. And like with Ed, she really didn't share those rough edges with me.

I figured that if they needed my help, they'd ask.

Axlam pulled her blue jacket tight around her frame.

"Got the new plow." I pointed at Bloodyhood. "So don't worry about your drive while the family's out running." Plowing wasn't something they needed to ask about, though. They lived about three miles up the road, on one of the other local lakes. Once it became clear that Axlam was as alpha as Gerard and Remy, the pack rearranged a bit. Gerard and Axlam built a big pack-ready house outside of town, while Remy stayed in Wolftown with most of the members.

"Thank you," she said.

"No problem." I nodded toward the car. "Can't help but notice you're little-wolf free." Even though Maura said there'd been a few moments of semi-disruptive behavior at school this week, I expected Jax to visit. He usually never passed over a chance to see Akeyla.

Axlam did the maternal version of an eye roll—that face I'd seen so many times in my two hundred years when a mother wished her child would get on with the process of learning a lesson. "Jaxson has not yet fully come to terms with his behavior, so Gerard took him to Duluth to pick up Remy for some quality alpha male time." She grinned and shook her head.

"Ah," I said. Remy must be flying in today. I was kind of surprised the elves had brought him straight home on a charter. But then again, that was Magnus's territory, and he was in New Zealand. "I hope I didn't make things worse," I said, "when I talked to Jax."

Axlam patted my arm. "You helped. He needed to hear that his behavior was inappropriate from an adult male of Akeyla's family." She glanced at the house. "Better you than one of the elves."

Her shoulders shifted under her coat. Perhaps she hadn't come to have coffee with Maura.

"The house across the lake," she said, "the one destroyed by that vampire who claimed to be your brother?" She never entertained the possibility of my brother actually being family. "It's owned by a lawyer, correct?"

She was probably here to talk about what happened with the interloper. "Aaron Carlson," I said. "He specializes in immigration law. His wife does intellectual property, I believe."

Axlam nodded. "What was your impression of him?"

"Arne put the fear of Odin into him. He also seemed to be an overall good guy," I said. "Honestly, I haven't talked to him all that much."

Axlam rubbed her hands together. "We may need him," she said. "The elves can work their magic, but they can't update Federal databases."

"True," I said. Modern mundanes and their technology had presented a whole host of new thorns in the sides of many magicals.

Axlam looked up at my face. "Do you have his contact information?"

This was about more than the pack, or the interloper at Raven's Gaze. "Everything okay?" I asked.

She patted my arm again. "We are trying to be proactive about mundane protections. That's all." She sighed. "That man, the one who lied about being a photographer and made the scene, what do you remember about him?"

So this wasn't a "that's all" kind of situation, after all.

The man had been a walking cliché. "He seemed too rich for his own good. Arrogant, too. He knew much more about the magicals living here than he should have, and like you said, he's a liar."

Axlam stared at the wine bottle gate longer than I expected, then inhaled sharply. "He felt... familiar... in the park."

Familiar? "How so? Like Old World familiar?" The wolves did sense something dark when he showed.

"We aren't sure, but the consensus among the pack is that he's involved with some sort of wolf magic." Her magic flared ever so slightly. "And with him vanishing immediately..." She shook her head.

The pack was as confused by his drive-by antics as everyone else was.

"I've been wondering if he was some sort of trickster spirit." Which didn't make any more sense than dark wolf magic, if I was honest, mostly because he hadn't seemed physically magical. "Though he presented as a mundane."

Axlam blinked rapidly for a brief moment, and she pressed her lips together. "He may never come back."

She sounded as if she believed the opposite.

If he was Old World familiar, could he be looking to settle some old French score with Gerard and Remy? But they'd been in Alfheim longer than the United States had been a nation. "If he's here to mess with your husband, he's fixated on some ancestral clan feud that should just be a story to him." The elven practice of living only one life at a time had more than a present benefit. It also released the quarrels of the past, something mundanes usually did by dying off.

Axlam's frown deepened, and her magic shook as if, for that one brief second, fear had crept in. She pointed at the sky. "Some strong spirits and other magicals can manipulate a mundane into becoming an avatar. The magic may have chosen him simply because he's fixated."

I thought about it for a moment. "I hadn't considered that the magic might be wielding *him*." It made perfect sense.

Axlam made the maternal face again. But she didn't respond. She pointed at the road. "Ed's here," she said.

Ed Martinez pulled his cruiser around, backed it toward the house, and pointed its nose toward the road without blocking the sedans or Bloodyhood. Our sheriff had an enviable spatial relations ability I swore not even all the elves could match.

The passenger side of his cruiser opened and his nine-year-old daughter, Sophia, burst from the vehicle with a huge bag in tow.

Sophia was in the other third grade classroom at Akeyla's school. They played at recess, but this was the first time she'd come over.

"Hi, Mr. Victorsson!" she bounced over to Axlam and me. "Ms. Geroux!" She held out her bag. "We're going to paint."

I glanced in the bag at the mix of real acrylics, brushes, and small canvases. "Looks like fun." I pointed at the door. "Go on in."

"Okay," she said, then to Axlam, "Your hijab is pretty."

"Thank you, Sophia," Axlam said.

Sophia hitched up the big bag. "Bye, Daddy!" she shouted, then trundled toward the front door.

Ed stepped out of the cruiser and set his hat on his head. "Howdy, Frank," he said, with a hint of Texas drawl, and hitched his gun belt. "Axlam. I'm glad you're here." He did a quick tactical scan of my house, garage, and surrounding trees. "I did some digging on that company our friend said was funding his photography, one Natural Living Incorporated." He leaned against the back fender of his cruiser. "Turns out they've bought up land around Alfheim."

"A neighbor?" I instinctively glanced toward the lake and the new lots dotting the shore.

Ed walked over. "Not in the town proper," he said. "Not yet, at least." He rubbed his neck. "Several farms in the county were purchased last year. Most of them on the north side, near the forest. They've been empty ever since."

Alfheim, like every town in Northern Minnesota, was within a quick drive of either state- or federally-owned parkland. The forests also made the wolves' run less conspicuous, at least in the summer. But with the storm coming in, and with Samhain, the pack would be running more along the edges of the woods, through farm territory. They were less likely to get separated that way. And the last thing the pack needed was a lost werewolf on Samhain.

Ed pulled his notepad from his pocket and flipped it open. "It's a shell corporation."

Shell corporations usually meant someone was up to tax evasion, or money laundering, or some other form of no-good behavior.

"It's not just one layer, either," Ed said. "It's inside other shell corporations." He flipped to another page. "I got the report this morning. They all trace back to a French property management company that does business all over the world. A Fils de Loup Administration." He pronounced "administration" with all the extra flare and strong *ee-oon* at the end that Americans did when mimicking a French accent.

"Son of the Wolf Administration?" Axlam asked.

Ed nodded. "Whoever is behind this is happy to obfuscate the money, but this," he tapped his notepad, "this here screams *I'm here to cause problems.*"

"Wolf problems," I said.

"I'm trying to figure out who owns the management company," Ed said, "but I'm running into an entire parking lot's worth of roadblocks inside the French legal system."

Roadblocks that were likely set up on purpose.

"It's him," Axlam said. "The photographer. The interloper." She waved her hand. "Why does he feel *familiar?*"

Ed flipped through his notes again. "The official background check will be sent to Dagrun and City Admin this afternoon." He tapped at his book. "The French company is the most conspicuous. Thing is, they're not doing anything illegal. Not even close. It's all on the up-and-up, even if it is suspicious."

Axlam stared at the wine bottle gate. "Thank you, Ed," she said. "Gerard and Remy will be home this evening. I'm going to talk to Maura and get Aaron Carlson's contact information." She turned toward Ed. "If you find anything else, text me."

"Will do," he said. "I have the town police watching for him. After his little shows on Saturday, he's a person of interest."

"Frank," Axlam said, "will we see you at the feast?"

She meant the feast at the Great Hall the night before the first of the two Samhain runs. I glanced at Ed. He tried not to frown, but it didn't work. Axlam sniffed as if she'd smelled his annoyance. Her lips thinned as if she echoed his frustration, and she squeezed his arm, too.

"No," I said. "I don't run." I'm not magical, even if I can see magic. I would only get in the way. My lack-of-magic made a good excuse to stay away from all the feasts, since the elves refused to acknowledge that I didn't enjoy parties.

Axlam watched Ed flip through his notebook. "I will make sure you get the full run plan, Ed," she said. "Our route, who's running with whom, etc. We'll start at our house, as usual."

His cheek twitched. "Thank you," he said.

She nodded to each of us, then walked toward the front door and the elves inside.

"What kind of dumbass broadcasts intent like this?" Ed tucked his notepad away.

He'd changed the subject. Axlam's promise of information must be enough for now.

"A dumbass lackey to greater evils," I said. We had a rich man in town openly looking to cause pain. "He reminds me of my father."

Ed's expression softened. I didn't know anything about his family relations, or his wife's, but I suspected he'd seen enough father-son interplay to understand the entire spectrum of human possibilities. "He thinks he's a god?"

When you live with magic, a metaphorical "god's gift" was very different from a literal one. And whoever was behind this might just have some godly—or god-like—help. "If Axlam is correct, he's enthralled by a dark magic."

Echoes of the deck doors opening rolled around the house. Happy kid sounds followed.

Ed nodded toward the house. "No Jaxson, I see."

"He went with his dad to pick up Uncle Remy," I responded.

"Ah." He walked back toward his cruiser. "All of Sophia's other friends are normal." He blinked. "Town mundanes." Then adjusted his hat. "There aren't a lot of magical kids in the school."

No, there weren't. Elven children were rare, and right now, Akeyla was the only little elf in her elementary school. The children of the wolves tended to be mundane or not obviously magical, and they, too weren't that common.

Ed adjusted his belt again. He pointed west. "I want to check out the properties owned by Natural Living Incorporated, and I'd like to do so with someone who can see what I can't."

He could have asked one of the elves, or one of his wolf deputies. But he was here, asking me.

He must have read my expression because he grinned and slapped my arm. "Get what you need. I'd like to be home before dinner."

I turned toward the garage to clean up. Going out with Ed would give me an excuse to stop in town and see if I could find an end-of-season deal on a replacement bike.

"Whose bike is that?" he asked. "Looks like a Flying Merkel frame. Too bad they painted it. They're much more valuable in their original orange."

I glanced back at the bike. I'm too big to ride, and never paid that much attention to brands, motorized or otherwise, but I remembered the name.

Ellie had a refurbished early Twentieth Century bicycle.

Ed pointed at the house. "Make sure you bring that axe of yours."

"Will do." Looked as if Sal was about to get her walk in the woods after all, even if it wasn't to find my mystery woman.

Time to look for the debris left behind by a bad wolf.

CHAPTER 10

E d and I hit five different properties along the northern edge of Alfheim County, where the elves' lands met the federal and state parks. All five were within the normal run territory of the wolves. All five owned by one of the shell corporations Ed had found —and all five were abandoned.

We found nothing. Sal had clearly been annoyed by something at our last stop, but when Ed got called out to an accident on one of the highways, he made me go home. "You can get yourself kidnapped by vampires or evil spirits or demons, but please don't do it on my watch, okay? We need you," he'd said.

Sal hadn't been able to pinpoint her annoyance, and nothing overtly magical had made itself known, so I texted Arne and Dag and came into town with hopes of finding a new bike.

The locals—and the tourists—liked Alfheim's lack of chain stores. No big box warehouse anything here, just artisans and several blocks' worth of shops along the city's downtown shopping district.

I parked in the small lot down the street from the bike shop, shouldered Sal, and walked the block and a half to the storefront. I would not normally take my axe for a stroll along Main Street, but not a lot of tourists were around now that the air had taken on the crisp scent of the approaching winter. Strings of lights decorated several display windows along with the town's all-out dive into fall, apples, Halloween, and the bounty of Samhain.

A bell tinkled as I ducked through the bike shop's door. Like most of the shops downtown, its floor space was a meandering maze of cut-throughs linking spaces inside multiple adjacent buildings. Several of the galleries were the same way and made shopping more of an experience than an exchange of funds for goods.

Arne said it added to the charm and ambiance of Alfheim. Mostly, it made finding an employee more difficult than running a search and rescue operation into Superior National Forest.

After five minutes of navigating around a display of snowboards and snow goggles, another of winter clothing, a wall of local art, and a table of locally-made soaps of all things, I found Sif the Golden standing on top of a ladder at the back of one of the shop's many halls as she stuffed boxes into a dark overhead alcove.

Sif the Golden wasn't an elder elf, nor was she particularly power-ful. She was, though, the only elf in Alfheim who wove her entire magical black ponytail into a rope of smaller ropes of braids, colorful cords, and silver and gold chains. Sif carried an entire jewelry box's worth of adornment in her hair, and even though she was one of the few elves who glamoured blonde, she rarely hid the extras in her tresses.

"Frank!" she called. "Hello!" Soft twinkling filled the air around her head as she climbed down the ladder, as if she'd woven in pixies tonight.

"Salvation! How are you, darling?" Sif extended her hand. "May I?"

A gleeful, affirmative response blasted off Sal, and I handed her over.

Sif held my axe as if determining the weight of the spellwork that allowed me to carry her. "Nice," she said. "Benta's webbing doesn't interfere with your balance, my love?"

A negative response followed.

"Excellent," Sif said, and expertly swung Sal in a tight circle, narrowly missing the display shelves. "You need to come by my place,

Frank," she said. "I'll teach you some axe-specific techniques." Sif taught self-defense—and belly dancing—at the Community Center, and knew her way around the battle end of any axe. She tossed Sal upward. My axe rotated blade-over-handle once, then dropped perfectly into Sif's grip.

"Sounds good," I said. "After Samhain?"

Sif nodded. "I'm running with the wolves this month." The small grin that touched her lips said she felt honored to be considered.

"You are one of Alfheim's best trail guides."

The grin turned to a smile. "Thank you. So you will come by with Sal? I will always make time for you, my friend."

Like Benta, Sif oozed a distracting sexual intensity. But unlike Benta, Sif didn't wield it as a weapon. If anything, Sif's sexiness was comforting.

"Of course."

She shouldered Sal. Guess I wouldn't be carrying my axe again until I left.

Like almost every female elf in Alfheim, she was stunningly lovely, and moved like a cat. Sif, though, carried an "everyone's free-love mother" vibe that set up an uncomfortable—and obvious—dissonance for a lot of mundanes. She didn't seem to notice, or if she did, she rightfully didn't care, and went about her business being the town's go-to trail guide, purveyor of outdoor entertainment goods, and teacher of elven mindfulness.

"I need a bicycle," I said, "and was wondering if you had any left-over stock."

She wiped her hands on a kerchief stuck in the back pocket of her jeans. "Let's see." She tapped her chin. "I sold most of my overstock last weekend. Big close out sale!" She waved her hand through the air to indicate a marquee sign, then motioned for me to follow her deeper into the store. "But I do have three or four units left. What do you need?"

"Something sturdy with good tires." I had no idea what size I needed to buy. "With a frame you'd find comfortable."

Sif stopped right in the middle of the narrow aisle between two racks of cross-country skis. "For a *lady*, Frank?"

"Umm...." I swear my cheeks heated. Me, the walking pile of stitched-together corpse parts, blushed.

"Yes!" Sif twirled Sal again. "It's about time. And you came to me for a gift? I am humbled. Your lady must be special to get a mode of transportation. A bike is the modern equivalent to a horse." She winked. "Anyone I know?"

"Umm..." I said again, because again, I couldn't get out the words I wished to share.

Sif stepped closer. She peered up at my face. Then she blinked, stepped back, and without another word, returned to leading me deeper into the shop.

Ellie's concealments had struck again, so I changed the subject.

"You haven't had any issues with our person of interest, have you?" I asked.

She waved her hand over her shoulder. "Thankfully, no."

"He seemed afraid of Bjorn, to be honest," I said, "and more interested in harassing mundanes."

Sif stopped again and her lower lip trembled just a bit. "How are Bjorn and Lennart?"

She was responding to my mention of Bjorn in almost exactly the same way Lennart had to my mention of Maura. Same set to her shoulders. Same looking away. Same touching of her ear.

I was beginning to wonder if I'd missed a memo about how this particular Samhain also landed on some otherwise-unknown elven season of love.

Sif laughed. "You know how it is, Frank," she said. "There are rules to the magic."

Yeah, she was an elf.

"Benta took up with me." It just slipped out. Elven pairings were none of my business, and honestly, I never really paid attention. I'd long been more concerned about my own broken heart.

Which was selfish. It was. But sometimes one has only so much space in one's world for other people's hugs and kisses.

Sif sighed. "And Maura took up with a fire spirit." She shook her head. "We are who we are, we elves." Now she shrugged. "We cannot argue with the magic."

And there it was, the elven equivalent of "It's in God's hands." But that didn't mean we couldn't fight the power. Fight the magic. Make inroads. Make life better for the one we loved.

Sal axe-snorted.

Sif glanced at my axe as if annoyed that she would interject, then pointed a finger at me. "You look confused, Frank."

You have no idea, I thought.

Sif chuckled. "Come."

I followed Sif and wiggled through a doorway proportioned only for the smaller among the elves into an also-too-small space full of overstock. Boxes filled every corner. Art sat stacked against the walls. Sif the Golden hoarded only the useful and the beautiful.

"Let's see." She handed Sal to me before moving aside a stack of containers full of winter hats and scarves. "Need new mittens?" she asked.

"Umm…" I said yet again.

Sif touched the side of her nose. "You aren't leaving until we have your unknown lady outfitted."

Sal agreed that the polite thing to do would be to make sure the unknown fae magic that kept coming around the house at least had warm toes.

Sif's mouth dropped open. "*Fae* magic, Frank? And do *not* answer me with an *umm…*"

Sal responded that it was nothing to worry about.

"Really, Sal?" Sif asked. She opened her mouth to ask another question, but just like before, stopped.

As did I, as if I'd run into a wall. Or the wall had run into me. Would I ever be able to talk to an elf about…

I pinched the bridge of my nose. Why was I here? "A bike," I said. "I have an old bike in my garage and I need a replacement."

We all stood there for an uncomfortable moment, me the crammed-in, forgetful giant, Sif the increasingly-annoyed-by-unknown-magic elf, and Sal the magical axe who wasn't really helping.

"Maybe I should come back another day," I said.

Except I shouldn't, because I should be fighting the magic. Because Ellie needed me to, or at least that's what I kept telling myself every time the concealments tossed a head full of confusion at me.

Sif the Golden stared past my shoulder. "Sure thing."

They were tossing confusion at Sif, too. How was I supposed to fight that? How was I supposed to make inroads when I couldn't even identify the undergrowth that needed clearing? How could I make life better if I couldn't make out a goal?

And whose life was I supposed to make better, anyway?

"I'm sorry for bothering you, Sif." I backed out of the skinny wedge of the doorway, Sal in front of me and the golden elf behind, and pushed my way toward the front of the store.

She continued to stare past my shoulder, but this time she looked out the shop's big display window. "Is Magnus back? That's a Tesla." She pointed.

Expensive cars weren't all that unusual in Alfheim. Aaron Carlson across the lake drove some German-built SUV. But Teslas were still uncommon.

It slid by the shop like a glossy black beetle on its way to destroy the local crops.

"Who blacks out their windows in Minnesota?" Sif asked.

Sal did not like the Tesla. At all. I latched onto the one non-confusing thing I'd encountered since entering the shop, and pushed my way out the door and onto the sidewalk. "What do you sense?" I asked my axe.

Something, but she wasn't sure what it meant. There were layers of interacting magic here and she still felt as confused as I did.

The Tesla whined on by and disappeared around the corner.

"I'll place a special order," Sif said from the shop's doorway. "How's that sound?"

"What?" I asked. I glanced at the elf watching me. She was talking about the bike, not the automobile.

My brain wanted to answer with another *umm* but I bit it back. "Thank you."

Sif's magic shifted upward from its usual low-level shimmer to a brightness closer to what flowed around the more powerful elves. "Alfheim is a land of abundance," she said. "There are those who wish to consume it."

Then her magic dropped back into its normal low level of shimmer.

The confusion returned—which meant Ellie's concealment enchantments had something to do with this moment. What, though, I couldn't parse.

Sif walked over and put her hand on my elbow. "Frank," she said, "trust your gut."

"I will," I said, and gave her a quick side-hug.

She grinned. "Text the store if you want me to add onto the order." Then she waved me on my way.

Sal and I strolled down Main Street, but the other decorated store fronts, the music store, and the bead place all, for some reason, wiggled at my sensibilities in a way not unlike what I'd just experienced in the back of Sif's shop.

My axe vibrated. She, too, found tonight's confusion disconcerting.

"We'll figure it out," I said, though I wasn't sure I agreed with my own words.

Sal didn't respond. We walked around the other vehicles in the lot, and opened up my truck. I tucked her into her pocket behind the passenger seat and started up Bloodyhood.

Looked as if I'd return home without a new bike, or mittens, or even a kitten for my niece.

I pulled out of the lot and toward home—and all the confusion that awaited me there, too.

CHAPTER 11

I sabella Martinez and her brood were waiting to turn onto the road when I pulled up to my driveway. I couldn't turn in, not with her crossover taking up most of the drive's mouth, so I waved her through.

She smiled and waved, and Sophia rolled down her window. "Bye, Mr. Victorsson!" she shouted.

"Bye, Sophia!" I called as they pulled out onto the road. The Martinez children all waved as they made their way home.

I parked, and gathered Sal. The sun had dropped below the tree line and a soft golden glow filtered through the last remaining leaves. A cool breeze moved off the lake. Acorns dropping from Lizzy's oak plinked across the rocks of the driveway like tiny hollow drums.

Autumn receded. Soon the beats would come from shifting ice on the lake—which meant I needed to finish cleaning the garage.

I rubbed at my forehead. The bike still needed fixing—or I needed to figure out how to actually order one from Sif's shop.

Damned concealment enchantments.

"How am I supposed to fix this problem if I can't get a firm grasp on the problem that needs fixing?" I half-called toward the trees. "I can't help if I can't remember what I'm helping," I grumbled.

The front door opened. Maura stepped to the threshold and leaned against the door jamb. "Who are you talking to?" she asked.

My elven sister looked tired, which made sense, since she'd spent the afternoon with two nine-year-olds. Her magic shimmered as always, though, and didn't look any worse for wear.

"Sal," I fibbed.

Maura shook her head as if neither she nor my axe agreed, but unsurprisingly let it go. "The girls spent the entire afternoon on the deck skipping rocks and painting." She moved out of the way as I walked into the house. "Sophia's got quite the arm." She mimicked a quality rock-skipping maneuver.

"She probably inherited Ed's eye." Her father was good with his sidearm.

Maura's face took on a look of concentration that said *it's more than Ed's eye,* but she didn't say anything.

"What?" I asked as we walked into the house.

"Nothing." She opened her mouth as if to say what *nothing* meant, but closed her lips and walked away, toward the kitchen.

"Maura?" I called. Why would she hide something from me? "Does this have anything to do with why your father hasn't brought Ed into elf-space?" Because Ed and his family weren't "regular" mundanes, any more than I was.

Maura shrugged. "It's complicated."

I followed Maura into the kitchen and set Sal on her bed, a blanket on top of the mounted cabinets opposite the sink. She was safe up there, and not obvious. She sighed and did her version of snuggling in for a nap. Mostly, she wouldn't talk to me again until I took her down, or unless she sensed a threat.

My axe was an excellent home security system.

"Complicated how?" I asked.

Akeyla, who sat at the kitchen table, looked up from her coloring book. "Uncle Frank!"

"Hey, pumpkin," I said.

She smiled and went back to adding blue shading to a flower.

Maura picked up the stasis satchel meant for Rose's notebook. I'd left it sitting by the phone, next to the extra cellphone I kept forgetting about.

"Lennart made this?" she asked.

She was trying to distract me from my questions. "How is it complicated, Maura?" It didn't seem complicated to me.

She nodded toward Akeyla as if to say *not now*, which didn't help, and only made me want to ask what was so horrible about Ed's daughter that Maura wouldn't speak of it in front of her own daughter.

This was clearly an elf thing. I crossed my arms. "To protect Rose's notebook." I nodded toward the satchel.

Maura waved her hand over the buttery leather, and the blue-purple shimmer of Lennart's suspension spell didn't respond. She flicked her finger and a subtle sigil appeared around her fingertips. Again, the suspension spell ignored her.

"Quality work," she said.

"It is," I responded.

She glared at me and shook her head *no* again.

I glanced at Akeyla, who kept on coloring happily. She hadn't heard my questions about her friend.

Maura wasn't going to talk about it in front of her daughter, so I let it go. "I think Lennart's a little lonely up there at the brewery with only Bjorn," I said, the stratifications of "arguing with the magic" be damned. I could, at least, fight this little corner of the magic's "wants."

She ran her finger over the leather again. "He's so shy," she said. "For a Thorsson, I mean."

I leaned close so Akeyla wouldn't hear, though I knew she would. "He wants Akeyla to come by and pick out a kitten." We couldn't talk about Sophia, but we could talk about Lennart.

Akeyla dropped her blue pencil. "A kitten?"

Maura glared at me again. "Bjorn's cats are special."

"I think you should invite Lennart over for dinner." I leaned against the kitchen island. "Akeyla and I could go to a movie."

"Can we get a kitten?" Akeyla bounced around the island and into the center of the kitchen.

Maura set down the satchel. "Not until we're settled."

She meant a place of her own that matched Akeyla's particular magical needs. "There are lots on the other side of the lake," I said. "You two are welcome here as long as you need to stay."

"I want a kitten!" Akeyla yelled. "They're fluffy!"

Maura pinched the bridge of her nose. "Not until we get our own place," she said.

Akeyla frowned. "Oh."

"Let's talk about it after the wolves run, okay?" I said. The last thing we needed right now was a fluffy distraction while we were sorting the latest set of problems. "Besides, we need to ask Marcus Aurelius, remember?"

Akeyla's magic swirled around her in a controlled, yet excited way. My niece was hatching a plan.

"Lennart and Bjorn may have homes for this litter," I said, doing my best to get ahead of whatever nefarious kid-idea was forming in her little elven head. "We all need to work together to make sure we do the best for the kittens."

At least Akeyla wasn't asking for a unicorn or a Pegasus-style flying horse. Neither of which existed, but one never knew with strong elven magic around.

"Oh," she said again. "I want to ask Mr. Bjorn. Can I ask Mr. Bjorn at the feast?"

"Maybe your mommy can ask Mr. Lennart," I said.

Maura glared at me again. "Maybe *you* can ask my *father*."

She meant about Sophia. "About the complicated parts?" I asked.

Would Arne answer my questions about Ed? Something told me that he would not, at least not until the runs were finished and we'd taken care of the interloper. But that little something was also telling me that this particular "elf thing" could very well cause us issues in the near future.

"Who wants spaghetti?" I asked.

Akeyla jumped up and down again. "I do!"

Maura shook her head and walked toward the refrigerator.

The satchel had been sitting there all week. Why hadn't I taken care of Rose's notebook?

"I'll be back in a minute." I scooped up the satchel.

Sitting under the bag was one of Akeyla's school notebooks. I flipped it open.

It was full of Ellie notes. Notes I'd written but did not remember doing so.

Was I angry with the enchantments? Resigned? I couldn't tell, but Maura moving the satchel had reminded me that I had a phone full of notes I'd looked at this morning, and Ellie had asked for her bike and a phone.

The bike needed to wait, but I could deliver the phone now.

I picked up the cellphone box. I also stuffed a fat marker into my back pocket so I could write notes on the box. The sun was about to set, and I'd better set out the phone before I forgot why I'd bought it. "Sal doesn't like the satchel, so I thought I'd put it and Rose's notebook in the garage."

Maura's magic jiggled ever so slightly. "*I* don't like that notebook."

None of the elves liked it, but Maura and Akeyla mostly kept their opinions to themselves because, I suspected, they didn't want to be crabby guests.

"It'll be out of the house and in the garage—on the hook in the back above the cooler." Best she knew where it was, just in case.

She continued to frown at me. "You should probably lock the garage."

I wasn't always consistent about security. Now, with Sal here, it didn't seem all that important. Besides, if the house was unlocked, Ellie could get in if she needed me.

Did she need me? "I'll be back in a moment." I couldn't remember, so I did the next best thing. I ducked into my bedroom to fetch Rose's notebook, and went outside to leave Ellie a message.

∾

I FOUND a photo in the satchel. A photo of me, on my deck. A photo that clearly showed magic.

I'm not one to swear. Swearing was seen as the antithesis of eloquence. Eloquence was something I cultivated to make myself less lumbering and monstrous. But sometimes the universe needed to be reminded that not everything it did was appreciated.

Rose's notebook didn't seem to care about the photo. It didn't give me a new special object, or even a hint of magic. The notebook just was, so I slipped it into the satchel and hung it on the hook.

I took the photo with me as I walked around my house to the path leading away from my deck. I set it on the rail and flipped open the school notebook containing my Ellie notes. I could take photos of each page, of notes that clearly showed anxiety about not remembering Chihiro's address. Of the kangaroo I must have drawn. Of the story about San Francisco.

That photo was in the satchel, which meant it had been dropped inside by someone, probably me. The plate was a daguerreotype with sepia overtones, but in color. And it was cocooned in magic.

Ellie had taken it. When I didn't know, but it showed me, if not happy, at least calm during my time sunning under a morning sun.

The one time of day I never, ever remembered Ellie or my attempts to find her.

I swore again. "I don't like mixed messages," I said out into the trees. Not that this message was mixed. If anything, it was as clear as the sunshine in the photo.

I set the photo aside and opened the notebook to the first clean page. Then I set it to the side also, and I pulled out the pen.

The marker would cling to the cellphone box's cellophane window. I scrawled *Chihiro's number and address are in the memory* across the plastic, then *So are mine.* I'd also had the guy at the store copy over my entire cache of Ellie notes.

Then I picked up the notebook. *I don't know what to do,* I wrote. Should I tell her how frustrating the clues she left behind were? When was the last time I talked to her? What did she need? Because I was losing my patience.

Your bike needs extra repairs. I'll find you a new one, I added. Then I set the box on top of the notebook of Ellie's information.

The night was clear, if cool. The phone and the book would be fine out on the deck all night. If they were still here in the morning, I guessed I'd have myself a frustrating moment of trying to figure out why I'd left them on the rail in the first place.

I capped the marker, tucked it into my pocket, and pulled out my phone. Best to add a note to my notes about why I left the notebook. I snapped a photo and added it to the app.

Shadows moved out in the trees. I'd better go in before the forgetting I never remembered descended on my poor...

I looked back at Akeyla putting away her pencils. Why had I come out here? We were about to eat.

I rubbed my frustrated head.

My phone buzzed. A message popped up. *You have not texted this week. I thought it best to check in.*

The name said Chihiro Hatanaka.

Who the hell—wait, the two kitsune in Las Vegas connected us. Chihiro lived in Japan and was helping me to...

I couldn't remember. I looked out at the lake, then back at the house. Why was I outside? It was dinnertime. Akeyla sat at the table with her colored pencils and I'd come out here to... What?

You're helping me with something, I responded. *I don't remember what.*

Concealment enchantments, she responded.

Enchantments? Had the kitsune set me up because they knew about our French interloper before we did? How did I get lucky enough to get this contact? *Are you a kami?* I asked.

Because if she was kami, I could be calling more trouble down on Alfheim.

Chihiro texted back an indication of laughter. *No, no*, she answered. *I am a researcher.*

Researcher?

The evening's reset has already happened, she texted. *I can give insight.*

I walked toward the house. *Insight is exactly what I need*, I responded.

I will do my best, Mr. Victorsson, she answered.

Finally, some good news. *Thank you,* I texted, and set about making the most of this random opportunity.

CHAPTER 12

About a year ago, Chihiro had stumbled into Ellie's concealment enchantments.

Ellie, it seemed, found a small measure of peace in places kami walked, and they'd met at a temple that day. Chihiro carried no memory of Ellie, but had felt a connection anyway. They'd come to enjoy the spring weather and the cherry blossoms. It had been a lovely day, but a chill had settled onto Ellie. She'd borrowed Chihiro's jacket.

Ellie had felt the return pull, the one that set off each evening's reset. She'd left Chihiro's company early, because the farther away she was from her cottage, the more unpleasant the move. She'd forgotten to return the borrowed jacket.

When Chihiro realized she did not have her keys, and had left them in a pocket, she'd run in the direction Ellie had gone.

The cottage, Chihiro said, must have been distracted by its nightly closing to the world. Distracted and metamorphosing into whatever it became when it reset, because Chihiro had walked right up to the front door.

If Chihiro could do it, so could I. I just needed to find the cottage. Or ask Ellie where she lived, which I had obviously never done.

Chihiro said that not once had she thought to ask Ellie about her home, or to follow, or to look for the cottage the many times they had talked prior to her accidently following Ellie. She suspected the hiding of location information was part of the concealment enchantments, and that I'd have to figure out a way to circumvent that bit of slight-of-hand, unless I, too, accidently found Ellie's home.

Which only served to increase my background level of frustration and to stir up more ineloquent, coarse mutterings.

But there was something else in Chihiro's story that caught my attention: She always felt as if a mirage trailed her after she left Ellie's domain. She'd gotten inside the enchantments. They hadn't rejected her. And from that moment on, a ghost of the magic walked at her side.

Mirages, ghosts, shadows... just like our interloper.

And Sal had sensed something similar out at the abandoned farm where I'd stopped with Ed—and from that Tesla outside of Sif's shop.

I could leave it until the morning, but sometimes magic stood out more in the moonlight. Plus we were within Samhain's aura, which might just make any mirages stand out.

Ed had gone home after dealing with the accident. No fatalities, thank goodness, but I still wasn't going to bother him tonight, though I did text him my suspicions about the Tesla.

Dagrun was the first elf to answer her phone. "I'll meet you at the farm," she said, and hung up.

I drove out and parked Bloodyhood in front of the farm's abandoned house. Dagrun would arrive shortly, but I had Sal and a good flashlight. I turned off the headlights and waited the moment it took for my eyes to adjust to the moonlight. Silver danced over the pasture and the fences like water fairies as the evening's frost reflected the moon. An animal—a fox or maybe a coyote—watched me from the grass between the house and an outbuilding. An owl hooted, and bats flapped and dove around the barn.

Winter breathed onto the land her first real exhale of the year. If there was a sort of nefarious magic here, I needed to find it tonight, before that exhale became the shrieks and screams of the blizzard that was on its way toward Minnesota.

I held up Sal. "You were annoyed the last time we were here, and not just by the ravens."

She responded affirmatively.

"Where?" I asked.

I listened to Sal's hum hoping to pick out some sort of directionality to her annoyance.

She pointed toward the big elm in the house's side yard. The tree shaded the little building, or did in the summer. This elm, unlike the ones in elf territory, had already dropped all of its bright gold leaves.

Nothing about the tree stood out. No obvious shadows crawled on its bark. No birds sat in its bare branches, either. It was just a simple tree growing where humans once roamed.

It had lost a limb to rot not long ago, and a large hole had opened about ten feet from the ground on the side of the trunk facing away from my truck. Precise animal magic drifted out of the little cave.

"I think owls nest there," I said to Sal. Owls wouldn't come near an inhabited home, and their presence added to the haunted local ambiance.

I leaned Sal against my leg and held up my phone to get a good photo into the hole.

There was an old nest in there for sure. A nest, and a shadow.

I swung Sal up toward the hole, and she quickly confirmed why she felt annoyed—the tree had a localized concealment, and one strong enough to affect the images on my phone.

I looked around. There might be a ladder in the barn—or I could back my truck against the tree. The bed would give me the lift I needed to see inside.

Low-slung headlights swung off the road and onto the drive to the farm just as I began backing my truck toward the tree.

Dagrun parked her roadster and gracefully unfolded from its interior. She didn't bother to glamour, and her icy, clockwork magic flowed outward from her like a cloak worthy of her title of Queen. Its edges crackled and jostled, as if the natural, frost-touched magic of this place wanted to add crystal ice to the boundaries between elf and land.

"Your magic is energetic this evening," I called.

Dagrun stretched her neck and rolled her shoulders the way a boxer readying for a fight warmed up. "Let's get this done. I wish to return to my husband," she said.

I chuckled and wondered if it really was some sort of elven season of love. Perhaps I should feel blessed for being allowed too much elven information.

Dag's multitude of silver scalp tattoos shimmered under her thick black hair. She still wore the intricate braids looped in and around each other across her head, and an extra smattering of silver beads dotted the ponytail she'd had at The Great Hall.

My elf mother exuded all of her grace, power, and beauty tonight.

"Thank you for coming out," I said. Dag sniffed at the air as if the birds had left behind an icy scent trail. "The ravens have been here," she said. "They were bearing witness."

"To what? Ed and I had been out looking at a lot of farms all day." Two magical ravens bearing witness did not bode well for the witnessed. "I was the only one here. Do you think the World Raven is up to something?"

Dag walked toward the barn. She stopped about ten feet from the building's moon-thrown shadow, and tossed an intricate, clockwork magic over the entire open area on that side of the building.

A fox-shaped sparkle appeared on the side of the barn, low down, next to the ground. It flicked its tail and walked on through. Several bird-sparkles appeared along the top of the door, and up along the roof line, each preening and calling. Mice and voles appeared next, along with a considerable number of deer, all moving through the open space. Crows mobbed the ground, and not one, but three coyotes walked through. Multiple owls swooped in. A moose family followed, and a small surprise pack of timberwolves.

No humans meant the animals had returned.

Then Betsy and Ross manifested directly over a spot about ten feet in front of Dag. Betsy landed first, then Ross. They each added something to the cache, then flew off again.

Dag pulled out her phone as she walked to the little hoard in the grass. She activated the flashlight, then poked around in the grass. "It would be unwise to steal from their cache," she poked a bit more. "They have a nice eye for lovely lake glass." She held up a rounded bit of pale green glass.

I walked over. Several bits of odd-colored glass—milky white, black, red, and some a soft, pale green—which all looked so smooth that it must have come from Lake Superior, a bottle cap from Raven's Gaze, what looked to be the remains of someone's earring, a chain of five paperclips, and what appeared to be an unpolished nugget of silver. The nugget wasn't any bigger than the nail on my pinky finger, and was more gray from tarnish than silver in color. It also held a slight hint of magic, which wasn't all that surprising. Silver had an intrinsic magic to it, which was why it was the preferred metal of the elves, and why it caused the wolves so much trouble.

Dag placed the glass back into the cache.

"Do you think the ravens have something to do with the interloper?" I asked.

Dag shook her head. "I've spent some time with them. Like I said, they're here to bear witness, not to cause harm."

Her response didn't answer my question, but then again, I shouldn't expect a straight answer about magical ravens.

Yet they were helping, and help from ravens could mean only one thing—someone was looking to back the magicals of Alfheim into a deal-making corner.

I'd already been down this path once, in Las Vegas.

Dag stood and patted my arm. "You're worried about the World Raven, aren't you?"

I nodded.

"Wise," she said. "They're not familiars, if that's what you're wondering. They're true ravens." She patted my arm again. "Thank you for not going off half-cocked about all this." She waved her hand at the cache. "There may very well be more going on here than the unquiet brought by the interloper."

Tricksters did like to complicate situations.

I bowed. "I have learned my lesson, my Queen." I was still worried, though, even if the elves weren't.

Dagrun's grin turned into a true smile. She pointed at the tree. "I take it you were attempting to reach something when I arrived?"

I walked her around to the back of the tree and pointed. "Owl nest. Sal sensed a shadow." I held out my phone. "Look at this."

She stared at the photo I'd taken earlier. "I see nothing unusual, Frank."

So the elves couldn't see the shadows or the mirages, much like with Ellie. "I see the same shadow I saw around the interloper at Raven's Gaze."

"Ah." She handed back my phone.

I held out my keys. "If you back her against the tree, I'll be able to see inside."

"You trust me with your baby?"

Of course I trusted her with my truck. "You and Ed," I said.

Dag took my keys. After a minute or so repositioning the seat and the mirrors, she expertly backed Bloodyhood toward the elm.

"Hold up," I called, and hopped into the bed. Dag smoothly finished her maneuvering, and stopped my truck under the tree with about four inches to spare between the sidewall and the trunk.

I leaned toward the hole and blasted the interior with the beam from my flashlight.

The owls had left behind a couple pellets, straw, and a lot of feathers. I picked out a big flight feather, and tucked it into my back pocket for Akeyla. But other than the remnants of an owl's daily family life, I saw nothing suspicious, or shadowy.

I swung Sal in front of the hole and got a jolt for my efforts. *Something* was in there. Sal felt it, even if I couldn't see it.

"Sorry," I said. "I won't do that again."

She huffed.

"I promise."

She huffed again.

Dagrun hopped into the truck bed. "Salvation is annoyed."

I stepped back. "Do you sense anything?"

Dag rolled her shoulders again, but this time, instead of cracking her neck, her fingers danced.

Multiple interlocking, spinning sigils appeared between her and the tree. They reached out—not toward the hole, or the truck, but to the frost coating the branches and the few remaining leaves.

Each small bit of ice floated into the air. The free-floating frost twinkled like a million tiny bells as it lengthened and brightened into sheets of moonlight.

Dagrun had created a miniature aurora of ice and night. "Extend your arm," she said.

I did as she asked. The aurora condensed onto my hand first, then up my forearm to just above my elbow. Chill shot up into my shoulder, and a real, honest shiver set my entire body shaking.

"Whoa," I said. "That's *cold*."

"You can tolerate it," she said matter-of-factly. "It'll be gone in a moment, so use it now, son. It should freeze anything trying to wiggle out of your way."

Two hundred years in Alfheim and I would never cease to be amazed by the wonders of the elves.

I stuck my hand into the hole.

Feathers crystalized against my touch. Bone-and-fur remains of mice and voles froze to the hole's floor. Straw became icicles. The damp splinters of the tree's interior hardened. And...

My hand hit a box attached to the edge of the hole at about ten-o'clock. It hung down into the opening and physically blocked a lot of the space. I pulled away my hand and looked again. Nothing. I felt along the same edge while looking. Again, my brain saw and felt only the tree. I closed my eyes again.

The hole definitely held a metal and plastic box.

"I think we have a camera trap," I said. "It's concealed."

I gave it a good tug, but it didn't move.

"A magically hidden camera?" Dag stepped closer.

"Sal," I said, "Do you think you can cut it off its bolts for me?"

She didn't like the idea of coming in contact with something she couldn't sense, but agreed to try anyway. Dag handed her over and I carefully placed her blade against the housing along the rim of the hole. I gave her a good whack.

The box dropped.

"Thank you, my friend." I tapped around in the twigs and owl leftovers until I found the box, and closed my hand around it just as Dagrun's spell melted.

I saw only the palm of my hand. I felt only air. But I *knew* I held the box even though it had completely vanished from my perception. "I hate concealment enchantments," I grumbled.

Sal blasted out an enthusiastic agreement.

Dag stared at my hand. "You're not seeing residual magic? An outline, or a shadow?"

"I don't think I dare move my hand," I said. Anything could happen. The spellwork could force me to drop the box. We might forget I'd even removed it from the tree, and then I'd have a concealed camera trap rolling around in the bed of my truck.

"Open the toolbox," I said.

Dag popped the lid on the box mounted behind the cab and pulled out the purple cloth Magnus had meant for Sal so she'd be comfortable when riding in the back.

"Are you okay with us getting your blanket dirty?" Dag asked my axe.

Sal did one of her mental shrugs. She understood that we all had to make sacrifices if we were to get rid of the much more annoying concealment enchantments.

Dag wrapped the cloth around my hand—and the box. I was definitely holding something shaped like a common camera trap housing. Rounded corners manifested under the fabric, as did the window through which the camera took its pictures.

"My gut tells me our interloper is responsible." Dag looked out at the boarded-up house.

"I suspect so." I slowly moved toward the toolbox doing my best to hold my hand as level and steady as possible.

"No one sets up one camera trap," she said.

No, they did not. "I don't think either of us is going to have a calm Sunday evening." I carefully placed the camera into Sal's toolbox slot.

"Looks that way." Dag hopped out of my truck. "If we have hidden camera traps out here, I want them found. I won't have the pack running in compromised territory."

I set Sal next to the tailgate and hopped out the bed.

Dagrun frowned like a monarch who knew that the strong emotions of upset werewolves would bleed over into the elves—and the local mundanes.

Which they would. Ed was right to be worried.

She looked away and closed her eyes. "I must return to my husband."

She may have overshared earlier, but no more. I could sense, though, that the Elf Queen and King were not simply honeymooning.

"I'll take it to Bjorn." I set Sal on my shoulder.

Dag squeezed my elbow, then walked away. I placed Sal in the pocket on the back of the passenger seat. And the three of us drove back to Alfheim—our Queen to her re-honeymoon, and my axe and I on our way to see the two thunder elves about a box.

CHAPTER 13

I had two elves and a werewolf in the bed of my truck. Bjorn leaned over the toolbox, one hand on the lid and the other hovering over the purple cloth, unleashing a torrent of his lightning-intense, richly-colored magic. Lennart squatted next to Bjorn's side as if reading the currents of Bjorn's spellwork as he added to his own stormy bolts and shudders. Remy Geroux squatted on the other side of Bjorn, sniffing at the air as if attempting to pick up anything the elves missed. And I stood next to the truck to keep watch so that we could work in peace, even though I'd parked the truck in the rear of the still-busy Raven's Gaze parking lot.

Remy, like his brother, had a density to him even though he was small compared to a lot of the local mundanes. I'd long suspected the solidity of the Geroux brothers came as much from their French trader heritage as it did from their wolf-ness, but in Remy and Gerard, their two modes of strength accentuated each other.

He didn't seem all that happy about returning to Alfheim. "Portia Elizabeth says hi, by the way." He rubbed at his recently-cut dark hair before tugging on his well-tailored shirt.

Remy Geroux had returned from Las Vegas well-groomed and better dressed than he had been going down.

Portia Elizabeth, his mate and the wearer of an inexplicable red magic, had turned out to be a good influence on one of Alfheim's alphas. She was another woman who deserved more respect than the magic world gave her. Anyone who could overcome their dark nature, manage an unknown magic, *and* survive Las Vegas was a goddess in my book.

Even if we hadn't gotten along at first. But she had been instrumental in Arne and Dag's ascendance among the Elven Courts.

"She doing well?" I asked

He smirked.

I chuckled and shook my head. "You two are going to have to figure out the long distance issue," I said. "You can't move there." He couldn't. Her innate sexual magic would turn him into a mindless mate-slave.

He sighed. "We all do what we have to for love," he said.

Yes, we did.

"Got it," Bjorn called out.

Lennart and Remy stood. Bjorn scooped his hands into the box and lifted out the purple cloth.

The glowing ball of magic encompassing the cloth and the camera trap was so bright I squinted. Remy twisted his head and grimaced as if the entire parking lot screamed with a shrill, high-pitched squeal. Lennart stared at the ball with wide eyes.

Bjorn jumped out of the back of my truck in one fluid, professional-athlete-worthy leap, and landed so gracefully the ball of magic floated jostle-free and steady. Lennart followed with his own spectacular leap.

Not to be outdone by the elves, Remy vaulted over the side of the bed and walked out of his landing as if he'd just finished up a quality massage.

Moments like this served to remind me who were the magicals among Alfheim's population and who was just a giant-sized, reconstituted mundane who happened to see magic.

"Bjorn," I called. "We need to check for other cameras."

He handed the ball of magic to Lennart. "Take it in," he said.

Lennart pulled his Bulldogs hat down over his ears, then wrapped his hands around the ball. He nodded to me, and walked toward their loft behind the restaurant.

Bjorn waved Remy over while he watched Lennart disappear into the kitchen gardens between the restaurant and the brewery.

Remy inhaled as if to clear his mind. "We're not going to be any help locating cameras," he said. "The concealments must be calibrated for wolves. I felt and saw nothing beyond Bjorn catching the enchantment."

Bjorn inhaled in very much the same way as Remy had. "That calibration alone is interesting information."

Remy's nose twitched as if he smelled something unbecoming floating in on the breeze. "This *is* dark wolf magic," he said. "Gerard and Axlam were sure of it at the park, and I agree."

Bjorn's nose also twitched. "We have one. We can use it to find others. We'll get this under control by the time the pack runs."

Remy did not look as certain as Bjorn. This running needed extra elves anyway—elves who would be as distracted by Samhain magic and a blizzard as the wolves.

And I had a gut feeling what that meant. "Bjorn," I said. "Anything that negatively affects the pack has the possibility of negatively affecting the entire town."

Bjorn rubbed at a glamoured ear. "This isn't a Dracula situation," he said.

Maybe. I hoped Bjorn was right. "Ed will do everything he can to protect the pack, the elves, and the town," I said. "But there won't be elves around to help. His family will be at risk."

Bjorn looked up at the sky. "We do not allow mundanes in The Hall." He spoke the words without any hint of emotion. I couldn't tell if he found this annoying, or if he agreed with me.

"I'm mundane," I said.

Bjorn laughed. "You are no more mundane than the wolves." He slapped my shoulder.

"Ed is the town monster slayer," Remy said. "He killed that

vampire, Bjorn. You were there. You saw what he did. I think that counts."

Bjorn shook his head. "This is not a simple matter."

Remy must have smelled indecision on Bjorn because he pounced. "The three Alphas of the Alfheim Pack formally request—"

"Enough," Bjorn snapped. A pillar of thunder magic rose off his shoulders and flickered much like Akeyla's fire. He turned his back to Remy.

Some mundane, somewhere, had caused enough of a problem inside a Great Hall that the elves of Alfheim had placed a moratorium on regular humans entering the magic.

Remy pulled out his phone. "I'm going home." He swiped at the screen. "I need to discuss this with Gerard and Axlam before we brief the pack." He swiped through his messages. He stopped on one, and his eyebrow arched. "The boy continues with his obstinate behavior," he said.

Which would make the feast fun for Maura.

Remy sighed. "Oh, he understands that what he said to Akeyla was inappropriate. He explained to his father what you explained to him, Frank. He knows." Remy put his phone back into his pocket. "He just needs to understand that she has just as much of a right to be emotional about this as he does." He nodded toward Bloodyhood's cab.

Bjorn shook his head.

Remy walked backward toward his truck. "At this point, he's more upset about being wrong than he is about what he was wrong about in the first place." He pulled his car keys from his pocket. "It's an alpha thing, and it does not take well to interference."

Bjorn remained silent.

Remy saluted, and walked toward his vehicle.

Bjorn looked over his shoulder, then back toward Raven's Gaze. "Those two ravens?" He pointed at the oak tree. "They don't like Arne." He faced me. "Our Odinsson elf." More magic lifted off his shoulders. "They love Dagrun. They're happier to see her than they are to see Lennart."

I wasn't surprised. "She said they were here to bear witness."

"Ah, yes." Bjorn gripped my shoulder. "Our King and Queen have their own distractions this Samhain."

I shrugged. "Dagrun mentioned as much at the farm."

Bjorn stared at the restaurant. "This is one of the few times in my long life that I truly wish for Magnus's presence."

"You can always call Benta," I said.

A hearty laugh rumbled from Bjorn. "I did ask her to cat sit, didn't I?"

Ah, the wonderful Mr. Mole Rat. "I do not understand how such long lived elves can be so..." I shook my head.

Bjorn laughed again. He leaned close. "What is the most universal trait among all the gods everywhere, my friend?" He swept his arm at the sky above.

"Besides power?" I asked.

"Besides power," he responded.

The answer was obvious. Every pantheon was full to the brim with gods who did not act their age. "They're all cautionary tales," I said.

"Close enough." He laughed again. He touched the side of his nose. "And we are nothing, we elves, if we are not aspects of our gods."

That they were. "Sif at the bike shop was asking about you," I said. If we were all subject to the whims of the gods, I'd continue to attempt those inroads I was reminded of at Sif's store.

Bjorn blinked. "She was? When?"

Sometimes I swore the elves were oblivious to the obvious. "This afternoon."

He rubbed at his sideburn. Then he snorted out a chuckle. "This is Arne and Dagrun's fault."

"What?" I seemed to be asking that a lot. Not *how* or *why*, but that incredulous *what* as if I understood nothing. I should probably admit that I didn't.

Bjorn grinned. "Perhaps I should offer Sif a kitten? I do not have horses."

I couldn't stop the resulting snort. If I'd had water in my mouth, I would have spit it everywhere. "I think she'd like that."

Bjorn's grin turned to a wide smile. He grasped my shoulder, squeezed, then pointed at the path to the loft. "Lennart and I will figure out how to break these concealments by tomorrow evening. We will have plenty of time to check the route."

Would we? Something told me that if it took us this long to find one camera, that even with broken enchantments, finding anything else was still going to be slow going.

Bjorn nodded, more for himself than for me. "I will call Ed. Let him know where the magic stands." He sighed again. "And as an elder elf, I will take your words of advisement to Arne." He rubbed his ear. "But do not hold your breath, Frank. You know our King and Queen."

Yes I do, I thought, but I didn't say it. Nor did I make the obvious point that Arne and Jaxson had a lot in common.

As Remy said, it was an alpha thing.

"Call me, too," I said, and pulled out my own keys.

"I will," Bjorn said. Then he nodded one final time, and walked away, toward the enchantments in need of breaking.

MAURA WAS STILL UP when I got home. She sat at the kitchen table with a warm cup of tea between her hands as she watched the lake through the doors. The warm, soothing scent of chamomile filled the room, and I wondered if she was on her second or third mug.

"Can't sleep?" I asked as I set Sal on her bed.

My sister glanced at me, then back at the lake. "Any new information?" she responded.

I pulled out a chair and sat down. "Your mom and I found a magically concealed camera trap. Bjorn and Lennart are picking it apart right now."

She set down her mug. "And you think the fake photographer has something to do with it?"

I shrugged. "No strong proof. But it was on property owned by a shell company that's associated with the company from which he supposedly hired the equipment."

Her body was calm, but her magic was not. "I would have gone out to the farm with you."

"What about Akeyla?" I asked.

Maura inhaled sharply. "She's going to be nine in two-and-a-half weeks. She can handle a few hours here by herself, especially after she's gone to bed. When I was her age, I was running wild amongst the oaks and the river rocks, remember?"

I remembered. She'd been born while I was away at college, and my return to Alfheim had been full of Maura, the wild child princess. "I do. But still."

Maura looked out over the lake again. "The worst thing we can do is stifle her. She needs to find her magic herself. We cannot find it for her. Not that Akeyla will be running the woods. Not until she can hold her glamour when startled." She tapped her own unglamoured ear. "It only takes me a moment to set up an alarm spell in case she needs someone. Plus I got her a phone. I was going to hold it until her birthday but Sophia has one and Akeyla's been begging."

Honestly, I hadn't even thought to ask. "Akeyla takes priority so I assumed you were pretty much always busy."

She exhaled. "The mommy job." She took another sip of her tea. "I don't know what Mom's thinking."

Why hadn't I made the connection earlier? Probably because I hadn't been around for the last making of a royal elf.

Elven babies were special, and from what little I'd learned in my two hundred years in Alfheim, making one took physical *and* magical effort.

Which was why, I suspected, the elves varied so much in their power and longevity. It wasn't just the mingling of DNA that made the elf, it was also how well the parental magic melded.

"Can I ask you a question?" One I'd thought too impolite to ask since her return.

She nodded knowingly. "Akeyla's father didn't turn abusive until it became clear his daughter was more elf than spirit."

This was the first time I'd heard her refer to Akeyla's father as abusive. "I'm sorry."

Maura sighed. "You know, some among us can feel the future. Not so much see what is happening, but feel the flow of the river, so to speak. In dreams and in meditative states, mostly." She set down her mug. "Not me."

I knew that some elves showed precognitive gifts.

Maura pushed back her chair. "So, my dear brother, will you help this mommy return to adult land?"

I smiled. "Of course."

She patted my hand. "Thank you." She took one final sip of her tea. "We'll get this interloper business sorted."

I stood and stretched. "You seem less concerned than I would expect."

She also stood, and made her way to the sink to rinse out her mug. "Samhain night makes the wolves vulnerable." She set the mug in the dish drainer. "Even our pack." She said it as if she didn't believe the wolves really did need the elves when they ran.

"True," I said.

She leaned against the sink. "Samhain thins veils and grays out lines that would otherwise be black and white." She stood up and walked toward the bedrooms. "That's why Dad offered Gerard and Remy help when they first arrived. Our job, on the run, is to refocus the blur, so to speak." She stopped on the threshold to the hallway. "We're good at it, Frank. We know how to read the wolves, and we also know when there are problems." She turned away again. "The run isn't what we should be worried about." She waved. "Sleep well, brother."

Was she correct? Were Alfheim's elves and pack bulletproof on run nights?

It wasn't that simple. It couldn't be that simple.

Life in Alfheim never was.

CHAPTER 14

I spent the next day with Bjorn and Lennart looking for more camera traps, spells, and random magic out in the fields along the edge of the federal forest lands. We found nothing, even though I carried Sal, and came in at dusk.

Their last request: I was to come to the feast tonight. I argued, of course. It didn't make any difference, and I ended up waiting in the lot for Maura and Akeyla, because I knew if I went in without them, there would be little-elf hell to pay.

Maura parked near the street, and I'd pulled my truck in under the trees on the far side of The Hall's real lot. Dag's ice-blue roadster was in its usual spot under the lot's central light, with Arne's brand-new eco-vehicle. The car was sort-of SUV-shaped, a shimmery, dark, blood-rich red not all that different from Bloodyhood's finish.

We might be rid of the vampires, but our new vehicles sure suggested bloodsuckers and war.

From her pocket behind the passenger seat, Sal reminded me that one should always be ready for battles, bloody or otherwise.

I chuckled. "You are a font of wisdom, Salvation."

She axe-sniffed and made sure that I understand how correct we both were.

I pulled her from her pocket. She shimmered in the blue halogen brightness of the lot's central light, and her glow came from our proximity to The Hall.

Maura, her face also shimmering from her phone's just-as-blue light, walked toward the truck with Akeyla in tow.

I opened my door, stepped out, and waited for my niece to take my hand.

She smiled big. "Ready, Uncle Frank?" Akeyla seemed determined to make my first return to elven space since my brother's attack the best visit possible. "Mommy says Ms. Martenson made lefse."

The elves loved their classic Norwegian foodstuffs, and Sue Martenson did make the best lefse in town.

She was also one of the few mundane spouses allowed inside elven space around The Great Hall, even if she wasn't allowed into The Hall itself.

And again, I wondered about Ed. I wasn't getting answers until I got inside, that was for sure.

Maura looked up from her phone. "Okay," she said. "With Magnus out of town, it looks like Bjorn will be running with Remy." She scrolled again. "Dad's running with Gerard. Mom's running with Axlam. Jax will run with them."

Akeyla huffed.

Maura ignored her response. "So, honey," she said to her daughter, "Because it's Samhain and we have that photographer who's been causing trouble, everyone's going to be extra busy inside."

Akeyla nodded.

"That means you stay with me, Uncle Frank, or one of your grandparents, okay?"

She nodded again.

Maura continued scrolling. "Lennart is running with Mark Ellis, since Mark's still new-ish, and it's Samhain." She scrolled again. "I'm running with Doug Martenson on the outside of the pack because, Dad says, Doug will see stragglers and I'm powerful enough to bring them back in." She nodded as if this was the first time her father had given her this responsibility.

"Congratulations?" I said.

Maura shrugged. She tucked her phone away. "Especially since Benta's running with Sadie Hill."

Sadie was the newest pack member. I wasn't sure when she was turned, but I did know she was a handful. I didn't know why exactly, other than she didn't seem to have the iron will that got most people through the change.

"Can I learn a run spell?" Akeyla asked.

Maura looked impressed. "Watch carefully when I'm with Mr. Martenson. We'll show you the spell that allows me to hear him when he's in wolf form and outside The Great Hall. How does that sound? We can practice after Samhain."

Akeyla grinned. "Okay, Mommy."

Such a spell might help Akeyla with her Jax issue. But we had more pressing issues, such as getting the wolves through Samhain.

"*Hmmm*," I said. "Did your dad forward that list to Ed?"

Maura shielded her eyes from the light's glare and peered at the exterior "door" into elven space. I could make it out from here, even with the lights and the headlights. Either one of the elder elves boosted its resonance or I was seeing a Samhain effect.

Maura nodded toward the door. "Did you know the weather amplifies transitional magic?" she asked.

I took Akeyla's hand. "No. Did you know that, pumpkin?"

Akeyla didn't answer. She watched a car turn into the lot.

The Geroux family was about to park and make their way into the feast.

"I don't want to talk to Jax," Akeyla said. "I don't like him anymore." Her grip on my fingers heated up.

"Um, okay," I said. "Let's go, then."

Maura frowned down at her daughter. "Honey, we need to—"

A resounding *no* rolled off Sal. She insisted that the boy wolf was to first apologize and show true remorse.

Small, aurora-filled flames danced along Akeyla's shoulders. They swirled in a semi-controlled, yet organic way, and jumped to the tips of her now clearly-visible pointed ears.

"Can I carry Sal?" she whispered.

Maura looked over her shoulder as Jax walked around their car and stopped next to his father. His young shoulders slumped, and he watched Akeyla with wide eyes, but he didn't come over.

Maura swung her hand in a small arc, then tapped her thumb against her ring finger. A sheer, ethereal magic plume formed behind Akeyla. It wavered like a cloth in wind, then settled onto her shoulders like a cloak.

"If it's okay with Sal and Uncle Frank," Maura said.

I had no say in this. Who carried Sal was her decision. I just happened to be the guy she currently liked the most.

Sal tossed out the equivalent of *only if you promise to be careful, young one. I am heavy.*

Akeyla nodded.

Sal's blade was wider than Akeyla's shoulders, and her handle thicker than her arm, but my little niece took her weight just fine.

Maura whipped out a second cloak spell, this one around the cutting edge of Sal's blade. Seemed both spells were to buffer Sal's sharpness, and to protect Akeyla's skin for her first time holding a true elven weapon.

She stood tall. Then she turned around and looked directly at Jax.

Fire danced from her hands to Sal's handle, and up to the big blade behind her head. And then Akeyla did something I didn't know she had the control to do—Sal's blade burst into flame. Not the magic kind only I can see, but real, bright, hot flame. It flared upward as if Sal had just breathed fire, and quickly disappeared.

Sal tossed out a smug, satisfied axe-*humph.* Akeyla, though, didn't seem any more or less satisfied by the display, just... stronger? More regal? She was most definitely Dagrun's granddaughter.

I couldn't tell if Jax responded. Gerard seemed impressed.

Akeyla reached to take my hand again, but realized she needed both to stabilize Sal on her shoulder. "Let's go, Uncle Frank." Then she walked toward the entrance into elven space.

I couldn't tell if Maura was amused, proud, or shocked at Sal's acceptance of her daughter. Maybe she was all three. I certainly was.

Gerard, Axlam, and Jax would enter through the "hotel" entrance where the elves had set up the equivalent of magical locker rooms. The Great Hall removed all glamours, and forced the pack into wolf form. The changing area kept clothing safe and clean.

I waved my arm and parted the magic veil between the real world and the elven glory on the other side.

Evening might have spread her violet shadows throughout the mundane world, but in here, she'd spread gold. Every dark space had a golden edge; every bright, an edge of silver. The sky above shifted from near-black violet dotted with stars to a firmament of borealis shoals and swirling heavenly fires.

The red oaks rustled. An owl hooted nearby. The air, though holding the chill we left outside, smelled crisp and fresh.

In the distance, the gold of the evening cumulated as the sunshine roof of The Hall, and lit the tops of the trees like a beacon.

Laughter rolled down the path. Chatter followed, plus a howl or two. The feast brought the elves and the wolves together. They were upbeat, but there was still a strained tone to the gathering's sounds.

The last time I'd stepped through that gate, I'd had an oily, low-demon-like rage stuck to my soul. One that, like so much of the other magicks sticking their icy fingers into Alfheim these days, had been concealed.

If anything, it had proved that yes, I saw magic, but not all magic. Natural magic drifted around everything in the world. Elven magic created structured lines and coiling sigils. Spirit magic danced. The kitsune version of kami magic wagged its many fox tails. Vampires gleamed like the predators they were. The werewolves were all wolf, all the time. And the fae... well, the fae were the fae.

But every form of magic could be twisted and hidden. It could be pushed so large I lost it on the horizon, or so small and thin I missed it in my peripheral vision. It could be worked smooth, or turned into a shadow. Or it could simply be rendered invisible.

I'd lived with the elves for so long I'd forgotten how they sheltered Alfheim from the corrupted magicks of the world. Except now it was getting in. Carried in on the back of the unsuspecting, or with my brother, tucked neatly into the crevasses made by the scars our father laid upon us both.

What did it mean? I wasn't sure. The world was changing, and magic with it. Was this new escalation a reflection of the mundane escalation of technology? Of humanity's unending horrors?

Something was coming, though. Something big. Because if escalation was anything, it was a harbinger.

Maura touched my arm. "You okay?"

I looked down at my fully out-of-glamour elven sister. She and her daughter were all things beautiful about the world. All of life's wonders, and all its power. And I was better by far for having been adopted into their family.

"When I came through the veil," I pointed over my shoulder, "I was hit by a feeling of foreboding..." I didn't know how else to describe it, especially with Akeyla, my axe on her shoulder and in small-warrior-goddess mode, standing right next to me.

Turned out I didn't need to.

Akeyla swung Sal down to her hands. Maura's safety spells coiled around Sal's blade like a rubber bumper, and this close to The Great Hall, they had taken on a solidity they didn't have in the mundane world.

Sal weighed a good thirty-five pounds, or she did when I wielded her, but in Akeyla's hands, she looked fast and light.

"I want to go to fifth grade next year," she said. She flipped Sal back up to her shoulder. "Then I'm going to skip sixth grade, too."

What veils had just dropped for Akeyla? Because she stared down the path with a look much older than her almost nine years.

Sal agreed with Akeyla's decree.

Akeyla looked up at her mother. "I want to learn *real* spells, Mommy."

Maura didn't seem all that fazed by Akeyla's comments. "Sure, honey."

Akeyla nodded her head as if she, too, had felt the foreboding I had. "Sal says when Samhain comes, and the veils are at their thinnest, sometimes the past and the future talk. Sometimes they tell each other stories."

"I didn't hear Sal," I said. Next to me, Maura shrugged as if she hadn't, either.

"She's practicing speaking to one of us at a time. She says that she needs all her skills and learning, too."

Maura obviously shared my surprise. Akeyla had moved way beyond my simple foreboding.

"Oh," I said, as Sal confirmed Akeyla's words.

So the past and the future were having their own feast, and we just happened to be in the middle of their conversation. "Can you and Sal understand any of the stories?" I asked.

Akeyla looked up at me, and a new set of flames danced up Sal's handle. "I don't think they're talking to me, and if I listen in, they might get mad." She looked to her mother. "No one should gossip, right, Mommy?"

"Unless you hear something important and you think you should tell an adult," Maura said.

Akeyla nodded in agreement. "That's what I did in the park. They were talking about that man so I told Uncle Frank and Mr. Bjorn."

"Thank you, honey," I said.

"They're comparing notes," she said. "Like we do in school when we talk about what a book means." The flames on Sal's handle vanished. "Let's go eat. I'm hungry."

With that, my also-escalating niece walked toward The Great Hall with my axe on her shoulder and her perplexed mother following close behind.

And me, her equally perplexed uncle, wondering if—with all my sense of foreboding, and the increase in hidden dark magic, or just the all-around intensification of harm done by the wicked somethings that had come our way—I'd just witnessed a real harbinger.

Something big was definitely coming our way.

~

PERHAPS IT WAS Akeyla's new Sal-awakening. Perhaps it was my proximity to The Great Hall. But that night, I dreamed.

In my manic, raging "youth," my body's death-like sleep held my dreams to their most basic state—practice with my clumsy fingers, memories of walking a path, or other simple coordination tasks.

I was, after all, not fully alive; nor am I now, but in my early days I thought less and responded more.

As my mind formed and I began to understand my hungers, my dreams shifted toward touching another with those clumsy fingers, or longing for an unknown woman I followed down a path, or other simple emotional processing.

I suspect that, like any child, I was growing up, except I was re-born into a hideous giant's body, which also colored my dreams. So yes, overall, my two hundred years of re-life had been filled with the most common dreams a man could have.

None of which explained why I dreamed that I sat cross-legged on the roof of Raven's Gaze Brewery and Pub, on my sunning mat, in only my shorts. No sun warmed me from above, only the soon-to-be full moon, but I squinted anyway at the brightness.

The air shimmered with heat mirages the way it does in the desert. The mirages also buzzed, the way mirages sing because a mind cannot handle that it is looking at an illusion and fills in sound effects.

Behind the restaurant, Alfheim's thick, impenetrable forests blocked all light as if I was looking at the dark lands of the Old World and not the pine, ash, and oak of the New. Out there, timber wolves howled. A red hawk and a bald eagle soared above the treetops. Squirrels ran the branches and a white tail buck snorted and hopped back into the trees.

Behind me, at the front of the restaurant, a blindingly bright neon sign blinked: Raven's Gaze Brewery and Pub, a Crossr...

The rest of the sign was under the edge of the roof. I could not make out what it said.

Around me, the warmth of the moon wafted off the black tar of the restaurant's roof. To my left, the door leading inside. To my right, chimney stacks.

And directly in front of me, no more than two arm lengths away, Betsy and Ross laid out one by one their pieces of lake glass—white, black, red, and pale green.

Betsy and Ross were not these birds' names. No, they were Ravensdottir and Ravensson, though neither of those names was correct, either. But they were significantly closer to the truth.

Ravensdottir clucked. Ravensson cawed. They bopped around their cache.

"What are you doing?" I asked.

Ravensdottir cocked her head. "When the wolves consume the sun and the moon, who will return the light to the world?" she asked.

Someone poked my shoulder. "Frank!" My real shoulder.

I startled awake.

Maura stood next to my bed with her phone in her hand. "We have a problem."

CHAPTER 15

Alfheim woke up with the city version of a headache and a dry, plaque-filled mouth: Someone had plastered posters all over downtown. Large posters covered shop display windows. Small posters greeted customers on doors. Several had been found glued to the sidewalks, and not one of the lampposts along Main Street had been spared.

Remy sent me several photos, and I promptly forgot about my strange raven dream. The elves and the wolves were frantically trying to figure out how someone could have gotten in under their collective magical radar. I was to check the posters for magical residue.

The posters varied somewhat in color, but not design. They all featured a blocky, modernist "Alfheim"—I had to admit that the art was interesting and the design looked professional—plus an equally modernist "Revitalization!" and a website.

The site had a whole lot of nothing. Parts slid, pictures burst forward, and icons moved and declared a bright and shining future. Colors danced on every page. But not one of the catchphrases said anything substantial.

I pulled into the same small lot I'd parked in when I'd come by Sif's shop yesterday, and parked Bloodyhood off to the side. Even here, someone had glued a large version of the poster onto the adjoining building, and instead of historic brick, I was greeted with a huge "Revitalization!"

The air smelled crystalline and just as dappled with proto-ice as the light was with gold and gray. A hint of the coming storm smudged the northwest horizon. We were in for a bruiser of a blizzard. Close examination of the poster revealed nothing, but the sun had yet to hit the lot, and the night's shadow still clung to the wall.

I shouldered Sal. This time of the day, I would usually leave her in the truck, but I suspected an extra pair of magical eyes would be appreciated, and the best place for me to start was downtown, where the posters had been layered on the thickest.

Sif was using a big razor blade and a lot of magic to scrape three of the posters off her front window. As I walked up she waved, set down her tools, and wiped her hands on her jeans. "Frank," she said. "Sal."

My axe did her version of cuddling up to my shoulder. She was afraid she'd be used to scrape windows.

Sif chuckled. "Don't be silly." She returned to scraping her window.

"Did you hear anything last night?" The downtown owners lived in the apartments above their shops. Sif did, and up and down Main Street, others were coming down from their beds to survey the damage.

She shrugged. "No." She returned to scraping. "Do you see anything?"

I peered at the posters plastered over the windows across the street. They'd covered at least five blocks of shops on Main Street, and hit Wolftown, too. "No one's alarms went off? No spells were tripped?" All those posters meant a lot of activity.

Sif wiped her hands on her pants. "I slept through the whole thing. Sigard didn't wake up, either." She pointed down the street at the tattoo parlor.

Three elves worked at and lived above the tattoo parlor, Sigard Tovsson being the most powerful. Two other shops within sight of Sif's also had elves. And the pack mostly lived in Wolftown.

Whoever had done this had come in under Alfheim's magical radar, which meant I should be seeing some magical residue.

I wasn't. I picked at a smaller poster glued to the lamppost outside Sif's shop. The corner lifted up, and I leaned over to see if I could catch anything at all backlit by the dawn's first rays.

"There's nothing here," I said. "No shadow. No magic clinging to the paper or the glue." I swung my axe close. "Sal agrees."

Sif leaned against the window. "There is no way a group of mundanes could have done this without magical help."

She was correct. No way could they have snuck in under the noses of so many elves. "What is going on?"

Sif tapped her fingers against the glass. "There was an elf," she said, "in the enclave where I was born." She stared out at the road. "He liked to offer hollow gifts to the women of the village. Mundane, elf, even a spirit or two. He'd make these grand, sweeping promises but they were all promises to himself." She shook as if the thought called up other, worse memories. "He was one of the reasons I moved here." She turned back to the window. "This feels the same, except it's directed at the entire town."

Maybe. Or the true target hadn't yet been separated from the Alfheim herd. "What happened to him?" I asked.

Sif didn't look at me. "He's dead."

The memory obviously caused her pain, so I didn't ask a follow-up. "I'll check a few more posters."

Sif peeled one of the posters off her window. "Frank."

I turned back toward the small elf with the golden glamour. "Yes?"

She opened her mouth as if to say something, but closed it and shook her head. Her magic contracted as well, and her normal shimmer pulled closer as if forming a shield around her body. "Be careful, okay?"

"I have Sal," I said. "I'll be fine."

"Oh!" Sif tapped her thigh. "After you left, I pulled up a couple of special order bikes for you to look at."

My phone buzzed. "Hold on a sec." I swiped it open. "It's Ed." And then into my phone, "Hello?"

"Open the site that's on the posters," he said. "Then get down to City Admin immediately."

"Okay," I said.

"I gotta deal with this," he said, and hung up.

I stared at my phone's screen for a moment, at the frustrating photo of Ellie, and realized how ubiquitously annoying life had been since the re-wedding.

I opened the site listed on the posters, and right there, right at the top, a video opened.

Some kid with a microphone was walking around Alfheim's empty City Admin parking lot. "We'll be starting our tour here, at City Hall," he said.

"What the hell?" I said. Alfheim was dealing with a threat, but one that didn't feel like a real threat. It really did feel as if we were dealing with loud pranksters.

Sif pointed at my phone. "You and Sal need to go now," she said. She didn't look frightened, but her contracted magic vibrated.

"If you need any help, or sense anything, call Bjorn or Lennart, okay? They're working on a spell that might break open whatever hidden magic we're dealing with here."

She nodded. "Go on."

Sal and I jogged toward my truck, and City Admin.

CHAPTER 16

I turned into the Alfheim Administration Complex lot. The thick, concrete buildings of the Complex sprawled along the road, and provided both the town and county governmental space. The Sheriff's Department shared space with Alfheim's City Police around the corner from Dag's mayoral offices, City Planning, and the main library.

Ten feet in front of the Administrative Complex's main entrance stood the hungry-looking young man who had been broadcasting on the website moments before. He wore dress pants and a jacket, and held his microphone in a way that suggested he knew what he was doing. A bored-looking guy next to him held a different boom mic, and an equally bored-looking woman with a new, expensive camera stood to the side. None wore identifiers.

They weren't amateurs, but they didn't have an uplink van, so they were most likely freelance stringers.

Which meant someone was paying them.

Ed leaned against his cruiser, which he'd parked in such a way as to block the best shots of the Admin building. He'd also turned on the cruiser's lights, which flickered an annoying red throughout the lot, also probably in an attempt to ruin as many shots as possible.

He'd also called Arne and Dag, and probably half the pack, and they were on the way. I'd just happened to show up first.

At least the crew wasn't from one of The Cities' major television stations. The last thing Alfheim needed was a celebrity reporter asking questions as pointed as an elf's ears.

Sal did not want to stay in her seat pocket. She didn't sense any magic, but she didn't like any unknowns walking around Alfheim.

"We can't chance one of them taking pictures of you," I said. "Bjorn said that some seers can read real photos. What if some witch somewhere gets a whiff of you and comes looking to start a war?" Because with the number of villains looking to cause problems in Alfheim, I pretty much expected some random fae-born witch to saunter down Main Street looking for an elven battle axe or two to kidnap.

Sal tossed me a clear *Fine*.

She, like my wayward dog, did not like to stay in the truck.

"Don't worry. If I need you, I'll come get you."

I didn't see any magic, but I hadn't seen any magic around our interloper, either.

The sun crested over the lower level of the east building, and a lovely sliver of golden light spread over the parking lot. The reporter pointed, and the entire crew moved to take advantage.

They didn't seem particularly professional. Their equipment probably cost as much as Bloodyhood, but they didn't really seem to understand what they were doing.

Ed noticed their attempt to take advantage of the light. "You three have been here long enough," he called.

As one, the camera crew straightened. Their shoulders squared. And they turned toward Ed's vehicle as one unit of semi-belligerence.

The crew wasn't acting oddly—anyone might be frightened by a police cruiser showing up at dawn—but the whole situation smelled too much like Saturday's wedding episode.

Ed stepped away from his cruiser. "I'm still waiting to see that permit," he boomed. He was in full authoritative police mode, complete with the frightening vocal inflection and the tense posture.

He must have had the same Saturday-morning thought.

The sound guy slapped at his pockets as if Ed's question had triggered some deep-seated, hypnosis-implanted need to give himself a pat-down.

"No permit. No filming," Ed said. "You need to shut down and leave. Now."

"It's public property!" the reporter-looking guy with the mic shouted.

They really were not acting like professionals.

Ed did not approach. He stood next to his cruiser, his hands poised at his hips, staring at the small knot of crew and equipment. "You still haven't told me who you work for," he called.

"We're..." The reporter sniffed and suddenly composed himself. "We can shoot cutaways and establishing shots."

The camera operator didn't pause. Her camera whirred to life and she swung it toward Ed.

He didn't respond, or act as if he'd noticed.

I opened my door. All three members of the crew frowned, but turned in unison to look at me.

"Why are you filming me?" I hollered.

The reporter looked as if he was about to stomp his foot. "Public property!" he yelled. "We're here for the announcement." He looked at his watch. "The cop doesn't believe us."

Ed looped his thumbs into his belt.

"Announcement?" I said. "What announcement?"

"I asked them the same thing," Ed said.

The sound guy fiddled with his equipment. The camera operator swung between Ed and me. The reporter looked confused. "The Revitalization Plan," he said. "The new community center. The clinic."

"Someone's been lying to you," Ed called.

I walked toward the crew. "No one in Alfheim knows what you're talking about, son," I said.

His cheek twitched. "Not our problem."

Headlights swept through the lot. Axlam pulled her sedan around and parked not far from Ed's cruiser.

Ed motioned for me to get between her and the crew. If this was a fake-photographer situation, she might be vulnerable to the shadowy magic we'd picked up around anything the interloper touched.

Axlam Geroux stepped out of her vehicle. She straightened her neon blue jacket and conspicuously arranged her City Manager lanyard and identification. "Hello!" she called, then to me, "Frank, come," and motioned for me to walk next to her.

"Did you get that?" the reporter said to the camera operator.

Axlam's wolf magic streamed off her toward the crew, then back to her body, as if her wolf was assessing the three people in front of us.

She smiled one of her huge, disarming smiles, and offered her hand to the reporter. "Axlam Geroux, City Manager here in Alfheim." She motioned to Ed. "Alfheim County Sheriff Eduardo Martinez." Then she motioned to me. "Frank Victorsson."

Her tone shifted when she said my name. Seemed I was to play the muscle. I clasped my arms behind my back and smiled at the crew.

The reporter looked shocked, but shook her hand. "We're here to introduce to the world Mednidyne Pharmaceuticals' new Rural Revitalization Initiative."

The only surprise Axlam registered was in her wolf magic's snarl. I saw it. Ed, of course, did not. I peered at the crew to see if any of them were picking up the new tension in Axlam's magic.

They were all as clueless as Ed, who immediately pulled out his notebook.

"I'm sure it's *wonderful* work," Axlam said without missing a beat. "Truly exemplary."

She had no idea what they were talking about. Neither did I. Neither did Ed, who continued to stare at the crew.

"Now," Axlam stepped toward the reporter. "I am sure you realize that these things happen slowly. There are codes. State regulations. You understand." She smiled yet again. "So there's nothing to film here today." She shrugged as if to say *Sorry*.

The reporter nodded knowingly. The camera operator continued to film. The sound guy now looked more confused than anything else.

"Please, before you leave," Axlam continued as if their leaving had already been agreed upon, "make sure you come in. It's early, and only a few staff members are here, but we'd *love* to sit down with you and your crew," she motioned to the camera operator and the sound guy, "and set you up with a tour of the town. Maybe stop at Lara's. What do you think, Ed? Lara's a good place to start for local color?"

Ed grinned more like a wolf than any of the pack ever had. "Best coffee in Northern Minnesota," he intoned. "Their food truck won at the Duluth Festival this year."

"We're a growing tourist destination," Axlam said.

The smile she tossed the reporter was as lovely as the other smiles she'd tossed out so far. But I saw her magic, and her wolf reared up in a clear dominance stance.

The reporter looked genuinely confused. He might not see her magic, but mundanes often sensed something when standing so close to an alpha. "About the Mednidyne Initiative—"

Axlam put up her hands. "State and county regulations," she said. "You know how it is."

"What was that you said? Ned-nigh-dyne?" Ed asked. "Spell it."

The camera operator gestured as if to say *cut!* The reporter frowned.

The sound guy's confusion erupted as a nervous tapping along the edge of his recorder. "I don't think he got a permit, Scotty," he said.

Axlam leaned forward. "He did not. But that's not *your* fault! Come inside. It's chilly. We'll get you all some coffee. You can tell us what your boss told you, and we'll get this all straightened out."

A barely distinguishable grin appeared on Ed's face. He put away his notebook.

Axlam shepherded the reporter toward the buildings. "Do you know about the resorts north of town?"

The reporter and the sound guy visibly calmed. The camera operator didn't seem to care.

Ed nodded to me. "I'm going to run this, what did he say? Med-nigh-dyne?"

I shrugged. I didn't pay attention to the world's mega-corporations.

Ed pulled out his notebook again. "It sounded nefarious."

I was about to agree when headlights swept through the remaining morning shadows. Everyone looked at the driveway—Ed, me, Axlam, and the crew—as a black Tesla whine-hummed its way toward the Admin Complex buildings.

Sal called out from my truck as if all the annoyance she felt about the hidden magic she'd been sensing since her awakening made her extra excited in a sort of itching-to-fight kind of way.

"That's the Tesla I saw last night," I said to Ed.

Axlam glanced at me as if she, too, felt Sal's call. "Stay here," she said to the crew, who were now halfway to the Admin Building entrance, and walked back toward me. "That's new," she said.

I moved closer so the crew wouldn't hear me. "No protection spells or extra magic." I peered at the Tesla as it slowly crept forward, moving in small, semi-halting rolls. Its nose turned toward the main Admin building, then the vehicle backed up slightly as if the driver was putting considerable thought into how best to park in the middle of a row of spaces so as to cover not two, but a full four.

Ed's lip twitched. He pointed at the camera crew. "You three. Go inside."

The sound guy immediately started for the door. "We only dealt with him via email," he called.

The reporter, Scotty, did not look happy about his sound guy talking to Ed.

"Go on," Ed said.

The crew quickly made their way inside.

Ed snapped a photo of the Tesla's plate, waited a second for the little beep indicating that the photos had been texted to someone, then tucked away his phone. "The desk will run the plate," he said.

Sunlight danced over the car's exterior, and even though it made me squint, it also pushed enough light through the blackout windows for me to see movement inside the vehicle. "He just dialed his phone," I said.

Axlam stared at the car. "What do you see, Frank?" she asked.

"With the sun, only an expensive paint job." No shadows, though apparently her magic sensed something. Her wolf had almost solidified around her body.

"I'm surprised he's not asking us to pose for selfies." Ed placed his hand on his unsnapped service weapon and walked toward the Tesla. "You know, for local color."

Inside the Tesla, the driver held his phone to his ear. He gestured with his free hand, then laughed.

He could just be a rich kid who was clueless about how the non-Tesla-and-yacht contingent of the world lived. Or he could be playing power games.

The driver continued to speak into his phone and, so far at least, wasn't moving around in a way that indicated he had a weapon.

"Ed," I said, just in case. I'd survive getting shot. Ed, probably not.

He stopped at the rear of the vehicle, but didn't look at me. He continued to watch the car.

I walked toward the passenger window and tapped the glass. The window rolled down.

"Frank Victorsson." I recognized the voice. Our interloper had returned.

CHAPTER 17

I stepped back and twisted my torso so the Tesla's door frame offered me some protection, and also so I could lean over and look inside.

The man in the driver's seat wore a rich person's casual clothes—a tailored t-shirt, leather jacket, and jeans that were much too clean and new-looking to have earned their distressed holes. A pair of black-lensed sunglasses sat on top of his purposefully messy hair.

"Power down all the windows and step out of the vehicle," I responded.

"When were you deputized, Mr. Victorsson?" he asked. He did not comply. He set his phone in a cupholder instead.

In my truck and too far away to help, Sal growled. Ed slowly made his way toward the driver's door. And I did my best to keep our visitor's attention on me. "Who are you?"

The man sniffed and rubbed at the tip of his nose as if he'd been snorting something unsavory. "I own the land you uncivilized barbarians have been smashing through these last few days," he said. "Did none of you see the No Trespassing signs?" He rubbed the tip of his nose again. "Tell your sheriff I wish to lodge a complaint."

Axlam took a step as if to come closer to his car. Inside, our interloper responded as if he'd seen her move in his rearview mirror. "I did this all for *her*," he snapped.

I held up my hand and shook my head. He clearly had an issue with Axlam. She frowned, but stopped walking.

"Why?" I asked.

He leaned over to look out at me. "Were you harassing my camera crew? Do you have any idea how much they cost per hour? This town needs a better attitude about outsiders."

Like at Raven's Gaze, I couldn't see any obvious magic on him, but also like Raven's Gaze, he wasn't well-lit. Good lighting would help me see any magical refractions around his body that might otherwise go unnoticed.

Ed tapped the driver's side window. "Roll down the window." He flicked the driver's side door handle but nothing happened. "License and registration. Now."

The man inside clicked his tongue. "It's locked." He looked back at me. "One cannot be too careful among those who lack discipline, correct?" he said.

Again with "discipline." I was beginning to wonder if he had a safe word.

"Ed," I said. "The driver is your person of interest."

The man sighed. "Please inform your mundane sheriff that there are only six fully-bulletproofed Tesla Model S automobiles in the United States. I own four." He smoothed his hand over the steering wheel. "I had this one shipped in from San Francisco." He leaned toward the passenger window. "For my time in this dangerous, dangerous place. One must feel safe while touring one's properties."

"You are in no danger here," I said reflexively without thinking about what I was saying, and the danger this man obviously posed to Alfheim's magicals. Subtle threats like the ones dripping like oil from his lips were a guaranteed path to elven retaliation.

The man chuckled. "Says the man with the magical axe in his truck." He grinned again. "So many things here might just jump out and howl at the moon. I prefer not to lose a limb to barbaric jaws."

"He just called the wolves barbarians, Ed," I said.

He pointed a finger at me. "Now, now. I most certainly did *not*." He sniffed. "I'm here precisely because of the wolves. I'm here to finish my father's work."

I slid my hand over the Tesla's iridescent paint as if the act would pick up some sort of magical residue. I saw nothing, nor did I feel any energy. "What are you talking about?" I snarled.

The memory card he'd carried at the park had a shadow. Sal was adamant about there being concealments here. And I was sure I'd seen the shadow at Raven's Gaze.

"When the time is right." He leaned forward and looked out the windshield. "Where is my crew? They have a job to do. It's time."

This man carried some sort of shadowy magical armament. It didn't emanate from him, nor was he carrying it on his person as protection spells. He looked like any other self-absorbed rich mundane.

Yet he knew all about Alfheim and her magicals, and he'd been mundanely buying up land around town for what Ed said had been years.

Years, I thought. This ugly little man who lacked his own magical abilities obviously had the resources to bulletproof himself—figuratively, literally, and magically. And he had an agenda.

And it looked more and more as if he was responsible for the poster vandalism.

"Your crew is smarter than you," I said. "They're cooperating."

His nostrils flared and his lips pinched into a mask of hostility. "They're fired!" He slapped the steering wheel. "Everything I do here is because of *her*." He pointed toward Axlam.

"He's a stalker, Ed," I said. A stalker with some sort of magical help.

"I am not!" he yelled.

Of course he didn't consider himself a stalker. He probably didn't think slapping posters all over window fronts was property damage, either. "Said every stalker everywhere," I responded.

He slapped the steering wheel again.

Ed tapped the window. "Roll it down!" he said.

The man slowly turned his head toward the shadow Ed threw onto his blacked-out window. "Does your mundane friend have a warrant?" he asked.

I moved slowly as I leaned down again, more to get a good look at the sun playing on the surface of the Tesla than to toss any dominant body language at our interloper.

And there, along the hood, the iridescence gave way to a shadow.

"He has cause." I tapped the glass of the car's rear window. "Downtown was vandalized last night. And you should really look into tint laws before you truck in an expensive car from California."

Ed tapped the glass again. "Out of the vehicle!"

The man gripped the steering wheel tightly and frowned. He obviously hadn't thought about the blacked-out windows.

"A fine is not sufficient cause to pull me from my vehicle," he said.

"Are you sure?" I looked over the top of the car at Ed. "Blacked-out windows may mean, what?" I asked.

"In Texas, we saw a lot of cartel vehicles with windows like this," he said loudly enough that the man in the car could hear. "Enough that searching their property fell within probable cause."

I couldn't tell if he was lying or not. But I wasn't the target of his bluff, so my reaction didn't matter.

The man's grip on the steering wheel tightened. "You need a warrant!" he yelled.

Something changed. The air, perhaps, or the angle at which the sunlight hit the top of the Tesla. Whatever it was, it pulled my attention completely away from the inside of the vehicle to its exterior.

And it... pushed me away from the vehicle.

Ed, too. His eye blanked—his whole body blanked out—and he backed away. We both sucked in our breath as if we'd been punched, and before I could blink, Axlam was between Ed and the car.

And the present Alpha of the Alfheim Pack broke the Tesla's door. I wasn't sure what she did, but it swung open and stayed open as if she'd damaged the hinge.

Ed staggered but quickly recovered. He drew his weapon. "Get out of the car!" he bellowed.

Axlam stepped aside as I rounded the vehicle. "Listen to Sheriff Martinez," she snarled.

I saw the glint of the weapon just before Axlam snatched it from the interloper and tossed it away from the vehicle. Her eyes shimmered with their golden wolf color, and she held her hands as if they were claws.

Was she about to lose control? I didn't know, so I grabbed the interloper by his collar and hauled him out of the car.

He balled his fists like a child. "How dare you touch me!" he whined.

I tossed him away from his car and toward a more open area of the lot.

All the hints of shadows, all the gleaming edges and the energy I needed to squint to see, erupted around him like a shimmering, bug-like carapace.

I wasn't looking at present magic. I *knew* what I saw wasn't here with us, yet I saw an echo.

Or perhaps it wasn't an echo. Perhaps he'd opened a line and I was looking at the magical version of a smartphone video chat.

The magic of Axlam's wolf leaped between Ed and the interloper just as Arne's own electric vehicle pulled into the lot.

Dagrun was out of the passenger side before the car stopped. She twisted as if dancing with the vehicle's door and walked directly toward the interloper. She said nothing, and her face communicated even less. She flicked her wrist.

A thick, semi-opaque wall of magic manifested between the interloper, Ed, Axlam, and me, but it did nothing to diminish his carapace of amber-tinted magic.

He jittered each time his shell pulsed, and his mouth opened slightly. His eyelids drooped too, as if whatever the magic was doing gave him great pleasure.

Dag did not disguise her disgust, and her wall pushed against the amber shell around his body. Sparks flew. She stepped one foot back as if to lean into a push.

And right then, right as the interloper tilted his head as if listening to someone whisper in his ear, dawn fully crested over the City Admin Complex. Bright, pre-Samhain sunshine flooded the lot.

The light hit Dag's wall, which expanded and shifted from her normal icy blues and greens to a bright golden shield.

Axlam's wolf rose up as a towering blue-violet canine energy. Hackles stood along its neck. Gleamingly bright teeth and a magical snarl erupted with such force I was sure the mundanes in the building felt the push.

Arne walked toward the interloper, his own wall in front of him until it merged with and augmented Dag's. "You will leave our town," Arne said.

The interloper pointed at Axlam. "She's why I'm investing in this pathetic little town! Why I'm bringing you civilization! It's my gift."

Nothing this man said made sense.

"I don't know you!" Axlam yelled.

"I'm here to right the sins of the past!" he screamed.

Axlam walked toward him, back straight and finger pointing. "Leave us alone."

The interloper threw his hands into the air as if asking the gods for help. "Why can't you accept the gifts I bring?"

Arne took Dag's hand. He stepped forward so he directly faced the interloper. Dag twisted so that her body was perpendicular to Arne's shoulder and the arms of their joined hands were flesh-to-flesh from wrist to elbow. Then Dag moved her free arm so that it, too, was perpendicular to Arne's free arm.

A sigil so dense it weighed on the air formed directly in front of them. They shifted the orientation of their hands—and released a blast of magic so strong the Tesla moved.

But the interloper did not. The blast flowed around him as if his shadow was some sort of shielding spell.

The interloper laughed, and his toddler-like foot stomping morphed into a neck-throbbing rage as if someone had flipped his nervous system's switch. He roared at Arne and swung his fist at Dagrun, even though he was more than ten feet away. "You'll pay for that," he shrieked.

Dag tossed a tracer spell.

The spell sparked and tried to attach, but his magic shell had an oiliness to it and the tracer slid off the pulsing carapace.

He shook his hands as if he'd been zapped by a battery. Then he bounced on his heels and howled at the sky as his shadow shell clarified and moved from static-filled to high-definition.

His carapace was filling up—or winding up. Magical energy accumulated and danced along its weird event-horizon edges.

He smirked like a child about to spring a trap.

He was going to blow up his magic like a damned flash-bomb.

I had him around the neck with my hand over his nose and mouth before he could yell or even bite. "Stop," I said. He'd hurt not only the elves and Axlam, but Ed and the mundanes in the building. He might hurt everyone in town.

He howled into my palm, but I held on. "I am the jotunn of Alfheim," I said. "This is my home."

I didn't know why I said *jotunn*. It seemed important, for some deep unintelligible reason, that I fake-out not just the interloper, but also his magic. That I pull a hand that felt, at the moment, to be much more than a joke.

The pulsing of his magic stopped. The carapace snapped down onto his body. The "call," it seemed, had disconnected.

I let go. He sucked in his breath. "I am going to make *all of you pay!*" he shrieked, and... vanished. His shadow flickered for a split second, then it too vanished.

I threw my arms wide, more out of instinct than any real ability to protect myself. "Is he still here?"

Arne swore. His augmentation of Dag's wall dissipated as his wife contracted her magic into a bubble around Axlam and Ed. Arne's organic magic spread out through the entire parking lot, flowing around my truck, the camera crew's vehicle, his vehicle, and the handful of other cars like a blanket showing all the lumps underneath.

He was trying to drop a sheet on our ghost.

"He's gone," I said. Quickly, too, since he'd gotten out of the lot before Arne sent out his magic.

Arne signaled to Dag. "I felt a burst of power." Then to me, "Did you see it?" He mimicked the headlock.

"It looked like he was about to explode," I said.

Arne swore again. He pointed at the building. "The camera crew is inside?"

"Yes," I said.

Arne jogged toward the door.

Axlam, and her wolf magic, stared silently westward.

Ed paced. "How are we supposed to protect Alfheim from *that*?" he asked.

Dag formed a sigil around her fingers and touched the inside of my elbow where I'd held the interloper. She then touched my cheek. "No residuals," she said. "The pre-Samhain sun burned him off."

"No," Axlam said. "Frank scared his magic."

"I told him I was the jotunn of Alfheim," I said. "And his shadow... hung up on him."

Dag, too, looked westward.

"His magic, it's *sent*. He's like you said, Axlam. He's using magic that's not his. He's an avatar." I rubbed at my hair. "It's as if he's walking around inside a receiver."

And I'd made him—and his boss—angry.

"Who's feeding him?" Dag, like Arne, spread a layer of magic through the parking lot.

Axlam closed her eyes. Her wolf retreated to her normal shimmer, but didn't calm. The shimmer continued to carry significant energy.

I pulled out my phone. "What did that kid say? They're here for someone's Rural Initiative?" Like Natural Living Incorporated, the other company might lead to some answers.

"Ned-and-Dine?" Ed said. He flipped open his notebook.

I swiped open my phone.

Damn it, I thought. I'd think about my mystery woman later. I opened my search app.

"Mednidyne," Axlam said. "He said Mednidyne Pharmaceuticals."

I tapped in the name.

KRIS AUSTEN RADCLIFFE

"The website's in French." I tapped at my screen trying to find an English portal.

Axlam held out her hand for my phone.

She swiped through a few pages. "Maybe there's a list of—" She stopped swiping. Stopped moving. Stopped everything and just stared at whatever she'd found on the Mednidyne site.

Dagrun walked over. "Axlam?" She touched her friend's arm and looked at the screen. "Can it be?"

"What did you find?" Ed also looked over Axlam's shoulder. "That's him, alright."

They must have found a photo.

"Bastien-Laurent St. Martin," Ed said. "He's the CEO?"

We had a pharmaceutical CEO menacing Alfheim like some second-tier trickster spirit?

"He's dead, Axlam," Dagrun said.

Ed pointed at the screen. "Wait. This guy's *dead*? Great." He stepped away and paced next to the women.

Was St. Martin like me? "I'm confused." I seemed to be confused a lot this week. Was someone else re-building people? He did own a pharmaceutical company. "Did you find something that will help us contain whatever magic he's using?" Was this all coming back, yet again, to my father?

Axlam shook her head. "Standing up to him just now was the dumbest thing I have ever done in my entire life."

Ed stopped pacing. "No. You did the right thing."

"I didn't have a choice." Fear crept into her shimmer, and her face. "He was going to hurt you, Ed."

Ed looked at me as if annoyed he'd needed to be saved by a werewolf.

She looked up at the sky. "St. Martin is bad, bad magic."

"Axlam?" I took my phone from her hand. And there he was, our interloper, grinning up at me like the entitled idiot he was.

I minimized the page and put his name into Wikipedia.

"He's not going to back off," Axlam said. Terror flashed across her face. Real, undeniable, traumatic terror as if that one phrase pulled up the absolute worst moment of her life.

I knew what that terror meant. I'd seen the exact same fear flash across Mark Ellis's face, and across the faces of other members of the pack.

This wasn't about rage. Bastien-Laurent St. Martin had somehow been involved in Axlam's turning. And that's also why St. Martin had felt "familiar."

"Dagrun," Ed said. He wanted answers as much as I did.

Our Queen shook her head as if to tell Ed to wait.

I scanned down through St. Martin's bio. He was born in the late eighties into a wealthy family of French doctors, and started Medni-dyne less than a decade ago after coming up with some miraculous drug for a disease I'd never heard of. There'd been a story a few years back about a proprietary major medical breakthrough. I didn't pay a huge amount of attention at the time, but I did remember the hoopla about the discovery, and their young genius of a founder. His past was mostly unremarkable, except...

"His father was murdered in a refugee camp in Kenya?" I said. The same year Axlam had come to us.

She hugged herself. "He was attacking kids," she said. "He'd already killed at least twenty-seven when he went after my sister."

Ed's mouth rounded.

"I couldn't let him take her. I couldn't." Axlam looked up at the sky. "He still managed to turn me before I stopped him forever."

CHAPTER 18

Bastien-Laurent St. Martin was the mundane son of the werewolf who had turned Axlam Geroux—a pathetic son who had found himself some sort of revenge magic.

In my two hundred years in Alfheim, I'd learned the stories of only a handful of wolves, and mostly in the vague, scene-setting terms given by Gerard and Remy when they left to pick up a new wolf. Things like "ambushed in Texas," or "the plane went down and a rogue wolf found the survivors," or with Axlam, "there was a werewolf operating in the refugee camp." That's all I knew, all anyone other than the people who went to gather her knew, and that was fine.

I would never ask. I would never pry. I had the pain of my own creation and I knew damned well that some things cannot be tossed around like a tale told at a party.

Axlam said nothing else, only stared at Dag's hand on her own. We all stayed silent. We all understood that such things were too personal —and traumatic—for most wolves to discuss.

She'd been young at the time—a teenager—and with her younger sister, who now lived in Minneapolis. She'd taken down an older, presumably stronger, werewolf in a Kenyan refugee camp before the Alfheim alphas and their accompanying elves showed up to help.

We were dealing with a vengeful mundane who might or might not understand that he was being used—and who, it appeared, was fixated on Axlam.

St. Martin probably didn't care if he understood what he wielded —or what wielded him.

"He thinks he's doing the right thing," Axlam said. "He thinks..." She inhaled and looked up at the sky, then closed her eyes and shook her head.

I knew what she was thinking. I'd met many mundane men like St. Martin. We all had. He even reminded me of my younger self—angry at my father, unable to regulate my emotions, targeting others who were easy to target because learning how to deal with those in power took effort and the last thing an angry young man who thinks he's entitled to revenge wants to do is to think things through.

Except I'd never hurt anyone. My father did that for me, then laid the blame at my feet.

From the look on Ed's face, he was thinking the exact same thing I was. "He'll get reckless," he said. "They always do when they get mad."

"That concealed camera," Axlam said, "it was along our run route." She motioned to the Admin Building. "He's going to come at us while we run." She sniffed. "While we're under a Samhain moon, when our wolves are strongest. When we are most likely to allow the rage of the wolf to surface."

"The pack will be safe," Dag said, in a way that suggested she found the whole idea of the elves not doing their job under the Samhain moon to be a great personal affront.

Ed ignored her tone and peered into the Tesla. "He said he was going to make us pay." He shined a flashlight into the interior. "That's a terroristic threat from an escalating person of interest." He stood up and faced Dagrun. "Crazy will do that, when it realizes it's visible. You have to move the run."

St. Martin had called us uncivilized. Axlam thought for sure he'd use the wolves' least civilized time against them.

But how? The obvious answer was to throw in a mundane as a werewolf snack.

Maybe the cameras had been a distraction. Maybe his appearances had been a distraction. "Any missing persons reports?" I asked Ed.

He knew exactly what I was asking. He looked at Axlam. "You *cannot* run here tonight, do you understand? What if he takes a trick-or-treater just before the moon crests the horizon? If he's going to toss a kidnapping into this just to see if one of the newbies will break, you *cannot* be here."

Dagrun walked toward Ed. "The pack has to run their established route. We can't chance a loss of stability with the blizzard and the Samhain moon. If we move north into federal lands, someone will get caught out there and we'll come home with frozen corpses."

Ed looked Dag in the eye. "If you stay here, we might very well have gnawed-on corpses."

"We will run as planned," she said.

Ed pointed a finger at the elf. "*My* job is to keep this town safe," he said. "It's the job *you* hired me to do. If the wolves run anywhere near town, there will be blood."

Dag's magic twitched. "We will not allow a mishap."

"Mishap?" Ed spread his arms, palms up, as if he couldn't believe Dag's words. "Someone *dying* is not a *mishap*."

"Ed..." Dag said.

"He said he was going to make us pay. That makes my family vulnerable. It makes all the mundanes in this town vulnerable. But there's nothing I can do, is there? You all put your spells and your magicks above everything—and everyone—else. How's that been working for you? Dracula got in."

"We took care of it," Dag said.

"Frank almost died!" Ed inhaled sharply and immediately centered himself. "When that vampire broke the wall between the Lands of the Living and the Dead—the moment he poked holes in structures that have supported this town for centuries—the dam cracked. I cannot fathom how you, Dagrun Tyrsdottir, the Queen of all the pointy ears around here, can justify ignoring the obvious."

For the first time in my two hundred years in Alfheim, I saw Dagrun fall silent.

"He wants me."

We all looked at Axlam.

"St. Martin. He's here for me. You said he's owned those farms for years. That's what the camera was for. To determine our protocols. Maybe for blackmail."

Ed shot Dagrun an angry look.

"He's been collecting information for *years*, Ed." Axlam said. "Years. It won't make a difference if we leave. He knows all our run territories. Who runs with us, their power level, who's new to the pack. Everything."

"He picked Samhain because he knows it's a magical night when you have no choice but to follow protocol," Ed said. "He showed up and made scenes so that we *knew* he knew. It's a terror tactic. He wants public revenge. He can't make the town's magicals afraid if we're surprised."

Axlam turned to Dag. "We need elves and pack at the schools. Make sure, when the kids leave, that an adult elf or wolf is with them, and that they go directly home, pack an overnight bag, and go directly to our house." She waved her hand. "Just to be sure."

Dag nodded.

Axlam turned to Ed. "That includes your family. They stay inside our wards until we get this under control." Then back to Dag. "Send someone to get Isabella and the little ones now. Make sure they stay with her at all times."

Dag pulled out her phone. "I'll send Sif."

"Ed, call a curfew. Blame the coming storm. Make sure everyone in town stays inside tonight and tomorrow night." Axlam rubbed at her cheek. "He seems... lazy. I'm not sure that's the correct word. Not so much lazy as unoriginal. My hope is that fortifying the routine will stop him from spreading his public revenge to the public."

Ed did not look convinced.

"He wants *me*, Ed."

I understood reckless men with anger issues. Men who lashed out like children, but weren't children. They were physically strong, or financially powerful. And too many of them took their revenge in fatal ways.

For the first time since Axlam had come to Alfheim, she looked small. "He's going to try to kill me first. If that doesn't work, he's going to try to kill my family and everyone else." She looked around. "So we make everyone else as safe as possible no matter how erratic he is."

She was right. The wolves were always right. And we had to find a way to stop him.

"We will find him," Dag said. "He will cause no more harm."

Ed still didn't look convinced, but he nodded and tapped the comm on his shoulder. "I need a crew outside to go over an abandoned Tesla." He waved away Dag and Axlam.

Dag touched Axlam's shoulder. A look of comprehension passed between them, then they both walked toward the Admin Building.

We needed a way to listen in on St. Martin's connection to his master's magic, or to track him, or to call him out in an isolated way, so the elves could put him in a cage.

None of which was going to happen before the storm hit. I looked out at the haze on the northwestern horizon—the blizzard was sitting over the Montana-Canada border, and the forecast had it moving this way at a speed no one had seen from a winter storm in a century of recordkeeping.

We had twenty-four hours before forty-mile-an-hour gusts full of ice and snow came scouring into Alfheim.

Behind me, in the Admin Building, Arne, Dag, and Axlam had the reporter and his crew under control. Dag would send out a few powerful elves to check the run's route.

"Keep an eye out," Ed said.

"Of course."

A deputy jogged toward the Tesla. Ed shooed me off and went about his work with the car. He'd issue the weather warning and the curfew later. We'd have a town full of angry trick-or-treaters, but better disappointed kids than dead ones.

As for me, I made my way home hoping I'd figure out a way to help.

I pulled out my phone as I walked toward Bloodyhood, to see if Bjorn and Lennart might want help with their camera-spying spells.

And there she was, looking up at me from my phone's home screen with her arms around my wayward dog. Ellie Jones, the woman I only remembered as the woman I couldn't remember but had vowed to find.

I almost threw my phone across the parking lot. I almost smashed it against the asphalt and stomped on it as if it were a bug wearing St. Martin's carapace of ugly phoned-in magic.

But I did remember that I should at least check my notes first.

Associate tangentially, the first note said. Not that it seemed to be helping. I scrolled through the rest about finding my way inside the enchantments, and about Chihiro Hatanaka, Ellie's friend in Tokyo. And about the bike in my garage.

There were several more about how she seemed sad when we talked, and how I needed to think through what I was doing with my need to find her.

And the one that said *Ellie knows Benta stayed.* I didn't remember Ellie, not consciously, but deep down some part of me did, and I knew I'd hurt her. Ellie, the beautiful woman who was obviously caring for my dog. And, it seemed, could have been my girlfriend if I hadn't been an ass.

My girlfriend.

And all those little twinges and pokes of attraction—all the magnetic-like pulls and the sensory focus and the energetic need to move—hit me hard. I had no memory of being with her. No memory of kisses or quiet moments or gentle caresses. No memory of acknowledgments of the attraction, much less intimacy. I had no reason at all to think such things were possible, much less shared.

Yet I did.

I did, and I'd let the wrong woman stay on a night I needed company.

I leaned against Bloodyhood's fender and stared at my notes. What had I done? The past was as big of a menace as the future St. Martin promised.

I scrolled down to the notes I'd added over the last few days: Ellie Jones was a seer, and I'd given her a phone.

Did I dare call after what I'd done? I watched the crew chatter happily as they walked out the Admin door and toward their van. Whatever the elves had done had fixed, at least for the moment, one small corner of our St. Martin problem. But he was random. Would he attack the wolves while they ran? Axlam seemed to think so. Were the cameras only for blackmail? Would he come after me while the elves and wolves were out in the blizzard?

Or would he go after Ed and his family, as Ed feared and Axlam wanted to halt?

He had said he would kill us all.

I called the number I had listed as Ellie's phone. It rang and rang, and went to voicemail. "Um, hi Ellie," I said. "I need your help." I inhaled. "My notes say you're a seer. We have someone in town who's..."

I rubbed at my cheek. Talking about magical things on the phone was discouraged, but something told me that I should be as clear as possible, especially since the odds of my remembering the call were thin at best. "His name is Bastien-Laurent St. Martin. He's the founder and CEO of Mednidyne Pharmaceuticals out of Paris. He's also the son of the wolf who changed one of our alphas. He's here to cause harm."

The sun spread warmth over my cold skin. "He's carrying access to a non-present magic. That's why we can't find it, and why I can't see it. Only its shadow is here. We don't know who is powering him, or what St. Martin will do next, and I was wondering if you could look and maybe give me a call back."

I closed my eyes and inhaled again. "I'm..." What should I say? "I found a couple other notes in my phone and I just wanted to tell you that I'm sorry. If you want me to erase what I have—if you want me to send them to Chihiro or do something else—just let me know. I won't..."

Could I let her go?

"I won't bother you again. But if you could help this one time, I'd appreciate it. It's not for me. I'll survive whatever he does. It's for Axlam. For all the wolves. For the elves. And he might go after Ed's family. I don't know. So if you could call back, or text, it would help. Thanks."

I hung up.

All I could do was try.

CHAPTER 19

E llie did not call back.

When the clouds rolled in, I figured I'd better go home and regroup with the elves. It sounded as if Ed and the city police had issued the weather warning asking that parents keep their kids in rather than trick-or-treating, so at least the blizzard had one beneficial effect. But there would be diehards, so Ed and the entire force would be in town tonight.

The sky had turned a steel gray by the time I pulled into my driveway, and the first snowflakes had started to slowly drift down. The air was deceptively still, as if the storm's icy humidity forced the winds to blow over our heads and not through the town proper.

The storm tugged at my bones and made my entire body ache, and I knew we were in for another Storm of the Century.

I set Sal against the wall just inside the door as I came in. The house was as quiet as the air outside, surprising since a second school bag also leaned against the wall. This one wasn't Jax's navy blue backpack, but a bright green with several charms hanging from the zippers.

Sophia must be here. Akeyla must have decided that she was going to be her friend's elf-guard for the night.

"Maura?" I called as I picked Sal up again. "Girls?"

"In the kitchen," Dagrun called back. She was leaning over a map on the table when I came in. "Maura went up to the Geroux place to augment the protection spells."

I looked out over the gray sky reflected in the lake. "Where are the girls?" I asked. They weren't in the kitchen. "Ed allowed Sophia out of his sight?"

"Isabella okayed her staying with Akeyla as long as they are supervised at all times." Dag nodded toward the deck. "Akeyla wished to stay here long enough to set a simple spell for your dog. She wants to keep your hound's food and water fresh during the storm. She's practicing with undergrowth off to the side of the deck." She waved at the door. "They're under a protection spell. I felt it best for them to learn and to feel confident rather than cower under a threat."

Dag didn't look up from the map.

"That's kind of her," I said. The girls weren't going to find my dog, but it was nice they were trying. I tilted my head and listened. Sure enough, faint kid chatter filtered in from outside.

"We are waiting for Axlam."

"Axlam's driving around?"

Dag looked up. "I warded her car, Frank." She looked as if she was about to roll her eyes at me. "Gerard and Remy are busy preparing the pack."

I'd obviously missed most of the logistics of the day.

Dag returned to looking at the map. "Akeyla refuses to go to The Great Hall. She says that as an elf who isn't running with the pack, it's her duty to protect the other kids tonight."

"That's..." Admirable? Problematic? I didn't know.

Dag stared at the lake. "We cannot argue with her magic." Then she shook her head and returned to looking at the map.

Sometimes the elves could be fatalistic. And right now, Akeyla's newfound need to exercise her elf-ness was more of a distraction than anything else.

Dagrun leaned against the table. "Akeyla will help augment the alarm spells. She is showing signs of her power. It's good for the children to hear from another child about the extra wards and the magicks involved." She flicked her hand at me. "Plus you will be there, as will Sal."

She said it as if we'd long ago set my agenda for the run—which we hadn't—and that my presence made all of Akeyla's proclamations just fine.

What if Ed needed help? Or what if … someone … called. I looked over my shoulder at the front of the house, as if I'd missed something when I was parking—just as someone else pulled into my driveway.

I rubbed at my forehead. All this with St. Martin, and the storm, and Akeyla—the whole thing was as confusing and frustrating as my time in Las Vegas trying to find Portia Elizabeth. Too many individuals asking for too much too fast.

For a second, I wondered if this was the new normal. How had my life gotten so complicated so quickly? But I knew the answer. When Brother cracked the wall between the Lands of the Living and the Dead, fissures spread from his points of impact in a fine, weakening web.

And webs draw flies.

It was a weak explanation and basically amounted to yelling at the universe for being mean.

"This pathetic little mundane will not hurt the pack." Dag ran her finger across the map. "He will not harm Axlam." She looked up. "I will deal with him personally tomorrow, after we finish the run. No one vandalizes my town and threatens my citizens."

Our Queen's matter-of-fact proclamation did not leave a lot of room for disagreement.

"Ed is right to be worried, Dag," I said.

She tapped her finger along one of the roads on the map. "Perhaps." Then she looked toward the front door. "Axlam's here," Dag said. She lifted her phone off the corner of the map roll and dialed. "Hey, honey, Uncle Frank is home and the snow's starting."

"Okay, Grandma," I heard. "Time to go in!" she yelled, loudly enough that I heard her through the glass door. I leaned into the table and looked out the side of the doors, and sure enough, two pink jackets moved toward the deck.

Dagrun pulled the phone away from her ear. "Time to go to the Geroux's," she said. Akeyla acknowledged, and Dag hung up. "I'll be setting up extra protection spells around their house, and I'll need to wait until their guard arrives, but we should check another farm after—"

My phone rang.

Ellie, it said.

"I need to take this," I said, but I couldn't answer. My finger wouldn't move.

It rang again. What was wrong with me? I was frozen.

Dag stepped around the table and toward the door...

And I could think. Damned concealment enchantments.

I jogged toward the front of the house in hopes I could catch Ellie's call before it went to voicemail.

CHAPTER 20

"Hello?" Nothing. I'd missed her call.

Damned enchantments. I smacked the front door, then swung it open and jogged toward the driveway. Maybe I'd catch her if I called back right away.

Axlam's headlights burned two bright white beams through the gloom and the gray. Huge snowflakes danced in the light as the increasingly-cold wind tossed them sideways.

The snowflakes would shrink in size but grow in volume as the storm rolled in. The wind, too, would go from its current brisk to a raging death wall of white.

The wolves would be out in this. Hopefully Ellie wouldn't.

Axlam cut the lights and stepped through the bright, swirling sigils surrounding her car.

Sif stepped out of the passenger side. "Hi, Frank!" She waved.

She must still be on guard duty. "The wards match the paint," I called.

Axlam stepped out and tossed me a *you're a smartass* look, then opened the rear door of her car. She leaned in, then stood up once again.

The saddest little wolf on Earth slowly exited from the backseat.

"He's here to apologize. We can't be worrying about the kids before the run." She looked around as if doing an Ed-like security check. "Not with what's happening."

"Mr. Frank," Jax said. "Will you come up to the house tonight?" He didn't add *so you can watch over Akeyla while I run* but the thought was as clear in his magic as one of Sal's head-pushed understandings.

Axlam's exasperation moved as a wave through her magic. She knelt next to her son. "What did I tell you at home? Akeyla is an elf. Frank is coming up to the house with us. He's going to be there with several other adult elves. Right, Frank?"

"Yes," I said. "Sal will be there, too."

Jax nodded. "Okay."

Axlam brushed a big snowflake off his shoulder. "Now you apologize to Akeyla. We'll be leaving as soon as Mayor Tyrsdottir is ready."

He twisted his head as if listening. "Akeyla and Sophia are on the deck. Akeyla is setting a spell to keep Marcus Aurelius's water from freezing in case he comes home."

Axlam looked as surprised as I had been when I'd come home.

"They're right next to the door, where Dag can see them," I said.

Sif sniffed at the air as if she smelled Dag's magic. "Our Queen has put in place a layered alarm, guard, and protection spell, but it's safe for wolves." She leaned forward so she was eye-to-eye with Jax. "I'll walk you through it."

He looked up at Axlam.

Some of Axlam's surprise subsided. She patted Jax's shoulder. "Go on, then." She watched Sif walk with Jax as he ran through the gate and rounded the corner of the house. "Let's hope this goes well and they don't go full *pon farr*."

I didn't catch the reference.

She grinned. "Never mind." Axlam turned back toward me, but stopped facing Bloodyhood.

I'd parked in front of the garage, angled so that from where I was standing in front of the house, I couldn't see the driver's side of the plow.

She pointed. "I think that notebook of yours left you another gift."

I walked around the front of my truck and there, balanced on the corner of the plow, were two photographic plates.

Ellie had been here. She'd stopped by, called, then left the plates when I didn't answer.

I snatched the photos off the plow and ducked around the garage. No Ellie. I jogged toward the path into the woods. No Ellie there, and no footprints.

I swore.

Axlam extended her hand. I handed over the plates.

"Ed gave Arne and Dag plates just like these after you vanished into Vampland. He said they'd fallen out of the notebook." She tucked one plate into her pocket and pulled the other out of its sleeve. "I was pretty sure at the time we were dealing with some sort of concealment enchantment. I forgot about the whole thing until now." She flipped the plate over. "They didn't come from Rose's notebook, did they?"

"No." Since she was in her less-magical human form, I could tell her the truth. "You never remember. It's part of the concealments."

She stared at the plate. "Samhain," she muttered. "Veils thin." Then she held it out. "What am I looking at?"

I took the photo. Bjorn's old church was on the left side, hidden in the trees, and Raven's Gaze on the right, with the big oak out front. In the lower left corner of the image, the top of Bloodyhood's plow blade was just visible.

"The woman who takes these photos, her name is Ellie Jones," I said. "She's been in Alfheim for a while. I'm not sure how long because I forget every evening. She must have taken the image two days ago, when I delivered the memory card to Lennart."

Bright points shimmered in the oak tree as if two stars had decided to perch in the branches, and had to be the two ravens. Elven magic hung like aurora fingers around the pub and the church. But what caught my attention was the layers Ellie had mentioned.

"She's a seer," I said. "Her stone takes photos of magic."

"A witch? The elves won't be happy about that, Frank." Axlam pointed over my arm. "These two points are Lennart's ravens?"

"Yes," I said. "This is elf magic."

I traced my finger over the most obvious, and prominent, layer—the greens, blues, yellows, and purples of the stormy magic I associated with Bjorn and Lennart. The area's natural magic mixed with the elf energy, and wove itself in and around all the trees and plants.

Nothing new or unusual. I was looking at the same magical world I saw daily, if brighter and more obvious.

This time, though, with the bright sun hitting the buildings and the magical build up to Samhain, other layers came into focus. Layers which, when I tipped the plate, were on different holographic planes than Alfheim's elf magic.

At the top, a soft shimmering of white sparks that looked almost like a veil. Under that, a second veil, this one colder, more wintry, and also just barely discernable. And sandwiched between the robust elf magic and the veils, one small, intruding pimple of carapace blackness contained to the walk in front of the church. Except in the photo, the carapace didn't look like a shell. It looked like an open muzzle of a dark, toothsome wolf.

"That's St. Martin," Axlam said.

I nodded. "It confirms that St. Martin's benefactor is dark wolf magic." But who? Or what?

Axlam pulled the other photo out of her pocket.

In the image, I stood on the path to the church in my re-wedding attire. Wisps of elven magic clung to me as they always did, but I wasn't the focus. St. Martin stood next to me like the little arrogant poseur he was, complete with his shadow shell. This close, it lost its wolf maw form and returned to the carapace I was used to seeing.

I tilted the plate. The carapace was contained to one thin slice in the photo's holographic layers.

"I wonder what that means," Axlam said.

"Dag might know." I re-sleeved the photo and put them both into my pocket.

"Come," Axlam motioned toward the house. "I don't hear yelling, but we still need to make sure the kids aren't fighting."

I patted the plates in my pocket. "We can figure this out when we get up to your place."

"I was hoping you'd come up tonight." Axlam squeezed my forearm. "Especially since Sophia is a sensitive."

A sensitive? "Is that why the elves won't allow Ed or his family into The Great Hall?" I'd think a sensitive would be better protected behind the strongest of the elven magic.

"They didn't tell you." She did not at all look surprised. "The elves no longer favor sensitives. There were problems before you arrived. That's what Gerard told me." She tugged me toward the house. "There are new protocols. No interference *at all* because of fate or something. Never mind that we are well aware of who among the pack's families are sensitives and could use a hand so they don't end up in therapy because they think they're crazy."

Axlam didn't seem any happier about the secrecy than I was.

"But she's Akeyla's friend. How is that not interfering?"

Axlam shrugged. "No interference also means allowing spontaneous relationships to develop." She pointed at the house. "Haven't you ever wondered why Arne tolerates Jax and Akeyla's fated mate magic? Even a less powerful elf could a put magical stop to their relationship without so much as breaking a sweat." She turned back toward the house. "It was spontaneous, thus protected by their no-interference protocols."

And here I thought Arne was being a good grandfather. "Should we tell Ed and Isabella?" He'd been about to punch Arne at the Admin Building. "What if—"

"Uncle Frank!" Akeyla and Sophia—with Jax and Sif in tow—pushed open the gate from the back yard. "We set out water and food for Marcus Aurelius," Akeyla called.

Jax looked lost, as if his big moment had been subsumed under Akeyla's work to make sure my dog had provisions. The poor kid was totally at a loss as to what to do.

"Grandma showed me how to set a beacon spell. He'll come home and we can ask him about a kitten."

Sophia, standing next to Akeyla, looked over her shoulder and around Sif. "What?" she called, as if someone was standing behind the kids and the gate, out of my and Axlam's sights.

Jax looked, too.

But neither Sif nor Akeyla looked. They had no idea Sophia or Jax were distracted.

"Jaxson!" Axlam called. "Who's there?"

Akeyla took Sophia's hand. "Grandma says it's time to—"

I heard a woman's voice. Sophia turned to Jaxson. "Listen," she said, and yanked Akeyla close.

I saw the person they were talking to. I saw her step in front of the kids just as the wine bottles of my gate lit up one after another as if a firefly pixie had teleported inside of each, one after another.

Jax's wolf magic burst out between the girls and the gate. Akeyla raised her arms in the distinctly elven way they do when they are about to cast a spell. And Sophia Martinez, the mundane nine-year-old friend of a little elf and a young alpha werewolf, braced as if she was about to get into a hand-to-hand fight with a monster.

"Kids!" I bellowed.

Axlam grabbed my arm. "Frank!"

The bottles shrieked.

Ellie and the children vanished.

CHAPTER 21

I spun Axlam to keep my body between her and the magical blast. Heat rolled around me—literal heat—and a crackling reverse electricity that danced as little pixies of static along Bloodyhood and onto the garage.

The magic turned everything into a negative exposure—the red of my truck turned green and the shadows behind the garage white. Even the static flickered as little black sparks and not the yellow-white of real electricity.

The heat and the magic were gone before I inhaled again.

Axlam wheezed and coughed. "Jaxson!" she shrieked. "I saw..." She rubbed her eyes as if confused. "Where is my son?"

The kids were gone, as was the woman who had to be Ellie Jones. All four had vanished into the thick air and the blizzard's rising wind.

Sif doubled over. She retched and leaned against the house.

The front door slammed against the frame. A wave of brilliant elven power burst into the drive and around the vehicles. "Sif!" Dagrun yelled.

Sif forced herself away from the wall. "That..." She leaned forward again. "That felt like a reset."

Dagrun roared. Whatever pain the blast caused Sif was also clearly affecting Dag, but Dag never showed weakness. Never.

"I will eviscerate you, St. Martin!" she yelled.

"He took the kids!" Axlam staggered to her feet.

"Wait, wait…" I was sure I saw Ellie, but I couldn't tell them that. Not with the elves this close. Not with Axlam's wolf magic manifesting.

"Frank!" Dag shouted. "That burst swept away *my* protections on the girls!" She pointed at the side of the house. "*Mine!*"

Had Ellie burst Dag's spell? But….

I rubbed my eyes in confusion. If whatever hit had been powerful enough to disrupt Dagrun's magic, we were in serious trouble.

A massive, bright sigil formed around Dagrun's arms and chest. It slid and locked, and a burst of power not all that different from what we just experienced exploded outward from her body.

I squinted and shielded my eyes. Her magic washed by me without doing harm, and rippled into the trees around the house.

She roared at the sky again. "No one takes my granddaughter!" she yelled. "We were going to imprison you for the harm you have done our wolves, but now you have touched the *royal blood of Alfheim!*" she shouted into the trees.

St. Martin took the kids? Part of me said no. Part of me said that they might well be safer than we were.

But that made no sense.

Dagrun's glamour ruptured. She didn't drop or release it, as most of the elves do when they step outside of their mundane disguises. Dag's pretenses literally parted as if her elven self had punched her way through her human chest.

"Frank." Axlam's voice had deepened and her eyes shimmered with her wolf. "I think that wave loosened her control. She'll hurt you or any mundane within ten miles if she doesn't calm down." She stepped in front of me even though she, too, was feeling the effects.

"Queen Dagrun." Sif held out her hands. "You need to breathe."

Big, fat snowflakes fell onto Dag's shimmering magic and popped with tiny wet smacks as if each one was a bug landing on a zapper.

"Dag... Mom...." I extended my hand to my elven mother. "I think that wave hurt you."

Her ponytail danced like a cobra behind her head. The jeans and tunic she wore wiggled and transformed into a magical version of her elven armor as if she had called the breastplate and helmet to herself.

And the Elf Queen of Alfheim morphed into an elemental magic I had rarely seen her show.

Axlam's wolf bristled. Sif stepped back as if the other elf terrified her more than the wave we'd just suffered.

"Where is my granddaughter!" Dag boomed.

Fully out of her glamour and in her elven armor, she pulsed with power—and manifested her goddess aspect.

She roared again. "You know not what you have done, St. Martin!"

Axlam leaned against my truck. "Get your axe, Frank," she semi-growled.

Was she turning? But the moon wasn't out. She was away from the pack. And the elf who was running with her was as crazed as an untamed werewolf scenting blood.

I darted for the front door. Letting either of them out of my perception probably wasn't smart, but neither was arguing with an alpha werewolf.

The door slammed against the wall. I'd left Sal against the wall just inside the door. I swung my hand down—and caught nothing.

Sophia's bag was where she'd left it, as was Akeyla's, but Sal had vanished along with the girls.

I backed out of the house. "Dagrun, did you move Sal?"

She howled more like a wolf than an elf.

I grabbed my coat, pulled out my phone, and dialed Arne. "St. Martin kidnapped the girls," I said. "Dag's enraged and Sif's hurt." I hung up, though I didn't know for sure it had been St. Martin, but Dag sure thought so, and I wasn't going to disagree with an elf.

Dagrun ran into the trees.

"We need you here!" I yelled.

Sif looked between me, Axlam, and the trees. "Stay here," she said, and bolted into the trees after her queen.

"Axlam!" I yelled.

"Jaxson!" Her howl turned into a full-throated growling yowl.

If she turned now, out here without her pack or Dagrun, this close to a change pulled out by the Samhain full moon, she'd lose herself to the rage her wolf must be feeling.

No human half of a werewolf could stand against that. Not even Axlam, Gerard, or Remy. St. Martin had taken Jaxson and Samhain was about to loosen all the separations between humanity and the magical underpinnings of the world.

The alpha wolf in front of me would kill every single threat, big or small, between her and her cub.

"Hold on, Axlam. Please." Axlam was fully capable of ripping off my arm in wolf state. If she lost control, she would be more of a danger to the local mundanes than Dag.

Her wolf magic vanished into her body. She bent forward. "He will not survive this," she choked out. "I will feast on hisss... hearrrrrtttttt."

I looked toward the house. If I got her inside, could I hold her until Arne got here? I didn't run with the wolves. I had no idea how to help.

I turned back toward Axlam.

Between us and well within my reach, Bastien-Laurent St. Martin, that little dung beetle of a humanoid, pointed the end of a large gun's barrel at my chest. "Quiet, now, Mr. Victorsson," he said.

"Where the hell did you come from?" I shouted. Quiet, I would not be.

He was in full winter gear, complete with boots, gloves, and an expensive trekking jacket complete with Mednidyne logo. His hat, though, said *Minne-snow-ta* like he'd bought it at a gas station somewhere between Alfheim and the Minneapolis airport.

Behind him, Axlam, who was still bent over, did not notice that St. Martin had materialized on my driveway. Nor, it seemed, had she heard me yell.

I couldn't see the magic he was using to separate us. Not really. Not with the snow and the wind. But *something* was between us and Axlam. Something that distorted the movements of the falling snowflakes just enough that my senses barely picked it up.

He'd put up a wall, or a veil, or had expanded his carapace-like shell of magic outward while he pointed a gun at my chest and rubbed at his nose like he'd been snorting his master's magic.

And all his erratic behaviors, all his delusions of grandeur, all the snickering and the harassment and the annoyance suddenly made sense. He really was a bug under that carapace, an unsubstantial rich kid with a revenge fantasy that made him the perfect patsy for something much larger than himself.

"You didn't think I would attack *turned* wolves while they ran, did you?" He shook his head as if we were all to be pitied. "Oh, *s'il te plait.* While they have the entire nest of elves with them?"

"Set the gun on the ground," I said. "Now." He had the upper hand, but I was bigger. Maybe I could intimidate him into cooperation.

He waved the gun around, but pointed it back at my chest when I took a step forward. "No you do *not*, jotunn." He sniffed again. "I want that one at her most savage." He pointed over his shoulder at Axlam. "How dare you reject my offers! I do *not* appreciate the disruption of my plans."

Axlam leaned against my truck. She'd calmed, and was coming back to herself. "Frank?" she called.

Did I dare swat away St. Martin's gun? I didn't have a good sense of his speed, and getting shot right now would hinder searching for the kids.

He pinched his lips like a blue-haired DMV matron. "Trying another headlock will get you killed, *jotunn.*"

He seemed to be fixated on the jotunn business. "Where are the girls?"

He twitched as if surprised by my question. "Your Queen and her under-elf? They're in the trees over there. I tossed out that *boom* to get them out of the way." He nodded toward the woods. "That Queen is knocking around like a bull in an otherwise pristine china shop. What is it with elves, anyway? Why the theatrics?" He rubbed his nose. "*This* is why your pathetic little town needs new management."

Axlam groaned. "Frank!" she yelled.

St. Martin nodded over his shoulder. "I was going to do this slowly. Savor my treats. It is Halloween, isn't it? Your American spawn dress up and demand tribute, do they not?" He did his little dance again. "But you had to go digging around on my lands." He waved the gun at my face. "You ruined *everything*."

"You harassed the elves at the park. You harassed me at Raven's Gaze." He'd spent the weekend running around town yelling *look at me!* And he'd come after Axlam this morning.

He bounced on his heels and rubbed his glove against his cheek.

"I have ten months' worth of photos of the Alfheim Pack. *Ten*. And you think finding that one camera made a difference?" He side-stepped. "I had a plan. A lovely slow boil. I was going to make this little town *so afraid*. Terrified! What is this horrid wolf magic that's come to our home!" He air-quoted 'wolf.' "Then you'd want my help." He paced again. "Need me. Pray for me. *Oui, oui*."

Did he even understand his own plan? "You are insane." Of course he was insane. He was some dark magic's pawn.

He cackled out a laugh. "She murdered my father!" he screeched. "*Mon papa*. He'd always bring me dolls from the countries he saved." He held the gun as if it were a toy.

"The elves can help you." Not that they would. Not after he'd taken the children. But he was insane enough the offer might get him to pause.

"*The elves can help you*," he mimicked. "The genie said you'd say that!"

Genie?

He worked for a dark wolf *genie*?

He pointed the gun at me again. "You be quiet, jotunn." He danced a little to side. "Jotunn. The genie didn't tell me there was a *jotunn* in Alfheim."

All this was because of a *genie*? A *djinn*?

"You got yourself into something bad here." I held up my hands and slowly moved toward him.

"Oh *no* you do *not*!" he shrieked.

I stopped.

He pointed the gun at Axlam. "I'm saving that murdering *bitch* for last. I'm going to put her in a cage in the City Administration parking lot. I can make the entire Alfheim Pack rampage that way." He rubbed at his nose with his gun hand, and thankfully, didn't point it at my chest again. "No one turns me down."

The nose rubbing suggested he was inhaling more than some genie's magic. The way he bounced on his heels meant he was distracted.

I snatched his gun wrist, squeezed, and slammed my other palm into his face. The gun, now pointed up, fired. My palm met granite.

Not granite. His magic shell.

And Bastien-Laurent St. Martin snickered.

CHAPTER 22

After the episode with my brother and the vampire quagmire that came with him, Arne believed we were about to face what he so wryly called "an escalation." He hadn't been specific about who he thought would cause said escalation, or what we were going to do about it. He simply shrugged and said that escalators were pervasive and a natural part of life.

Escalation was what got Remy and me sent to Las Vegas. Alfheim, with her welcoming enclave and her healthy and wealthy werewolf pack, was on many a magical radar. Alfheim was "modern," and being modern meant that you got all the perks and pits of the modern world —cellphones, electric cars, Cold War vampires who were really the ultimate Old World villains, and an ever-escalating crew of bastards with also-escalating weapons who thought they could take Alfheim down a peg or two.

I had one such weapon by the neck and gun wrist. The smug little toad sneered even though I had the upper hand and he was nothing but a tool.

"Who do you work for?" I demanded. "Axlam!" I bellowed. "Get Dagrun!"

St. Martin rolled his eyes. "She can't heeeaaaarrrrr yooooouuuu," he sing-songed. "You aren't the brightest of the elves' pets, are you?"

She didn't hear me, not directly—but her magic noticed.

St. Martin twitched. He tried to wiggle to look at Axlam but I held him—not him, but his shell—tightly.

Her eyes were still golden. She hunched, too. Her wolf wanted out into the physical world. Sending her off to find the elves like this was dangerous—but so was keeping her within St. Martin's reach.

"Axlam! Go!" I yelled.

If she was going to fall to these magicks, she would have already. But she was alpha, and she stood against St. Martin and Samhain's pushes and pulls on the veils. She'd get Dagrun and return.

She sniffed the air more like Marcus Aurelius than a person, and let out the closest thing to a wolf howl a human throat could make.

Then Axlam Geroux ran into the woods along the same path as our Queen.

"I'm going to pluck out her eyeballs!" St. Martin screeched. He tried to kick me, but I continued to hold him far enough away that he couldn't do real damage.

I might not have been able to knock the gun from St. Martin's hand, but I held his wrist in a way that kept it aimed away from my body. I could not feel his skin, but I did have him by the throat.

The sniveling toad snickered. "Won't do her any good to run."

"I could snap your neck," I responded, "and take care of the problem once and for all."

He sniffed again. "No, you cannot," he said. "And even if you could, you wouldn't. You have standards."

He was correct that I wouldn't kill him. If he died, we might never learn whose magic he wielded, and that would for sure come back to bite Alfheim.

"Perhaps I should snap your collarbones instead." I stared down at his puckered face without releasing his neck or his hand. I might not break a bone now, but he needed to understand that I would the moment we moved beyond this impasse.

"So violent!" He snickered again. "More proof this town needs discipline."

Not even the vampires had been this insipid.

A distant scream of a siren filtered through the trees. Ed was close by.

I lifted St. Martin off the ground by his neck and spun us around so I could get a better view of any vehicle coming down my driveway.

My house vanished. My garage, too, and Bloodyhood. Axlam's car. I changed our angle to the world and we were in the woods, between trees I did not recognize, yet under the same blizzard-filled sky and among the same blowing snow.

My deck—my *house*—was gone. The lake, too. No temperature changes. No real wind change, either. Just a move into the trees.

The snow fell in sheets of blinding crystals and the wind howled as if he had moved us into the heart of the blizzard, and I was not near my home.

I shook St. Martin. "What did you do?" There hadn't been a burst of magic like when he stole the kids, or any sign that he'd moved us into a pocket land. My house might still be there. The trees could be an illusion.

He snickered as he dangled from my hand.

"Threatening Alfheim will fast-track you into a permanent, uncomfortable, elf-controlled existence," I said.

He gulped and slapped at my arm. The granite-hard shell around his fingers stung but he wasn't nearly strong enough to do real damage. "Those little girls giggling on your deck looked tasty," he croaked out. "My, grandma, what big ears you have."

He said *those little girls on your deck* as if he'd planned to take them, but hadn't.

Something was wrong—obviously the situation was wrong, but I was beginning to wonder if there was another unknown force at work here.

"Your boss. I want a name." He did not have a real genie on his side. He was too inept with his planning and his posturing. "I want locations of all spells meant to harm the wolves." But then again, genies did like the incompetent. "And I want the children returned. *Now.*"

He slapped at my wrist again, and tried to pull away his gun hand. "Put me down, you pathetic monster. Nobody loves you. Never have. Never will."

I gave him a good shake. "Your shell is keeping me from pressing into your skin." I rolled my shoulder outward and used every muscle in my back and arm to crank his gun hand to the side.

He shrieked.

"Yet overpowering your bones is such a simple matter," I said.

"She killed my father!" he yelled. "Bitch needs to be taught her place!" No threats toward the children, only his predictable and pathetic daddy issues.

I yanked him close so he'd feel my breath. "This stops now. Do you understand, insect?"

"I'm going to catch the Sheriff's girl," he croaked out. "I'm going to catch that little elf and that puppy of hers. I'm going to put that murderer in a cage and I'm going to feed her those children one at a time. That's what you all fear, isn't it? That the true nature of the wolf will overtake the Alfheim Pack? And that the elves won't be able to stop the resulting dismemberment?"

He spit. It hit my cheek like it had already frozen.

"That's why my genie said to plan. That's why he said to chip away at their mundane protections!" He swung his legs and tried to push me away with his feet.

It didn't work.

"I'll call those American immigration police!" he croaked out. "The ones who take babies without *any* dark magical help!"

He was using every possible attack—magical and mundane. And if he really did work for a genie—or a genie worked for him—he literally had access to chaos.

Chaos magic explained his erratic behavior. It explained the unpredictability and the ability to slam sideways into Alfheim like an eighteen-wheeler crossing a highway.

"What's your special town going to do when they show up just as the pack is changing to run the blizzard? What are you going to do when they find that bitch with blood in her mouth and the torn-apart bodies of Alfheim's sweetest little ones?"

All I needed to do was crack his shell. I could snap a few bones and render him unconscious.

And pray his benefactor didn't have other tentacles into Alfheim—which it might. St. Martin did not seem to understand that the kids were already gone, or that all of them had been taken, not just those closest to Axlam. That might have happened without him knowing.

I swung him around and slammed his back into a tree hard enough to break his spine.

He croaked out a laugh. "My genie made special arrangements for you, jotunn!" he yipped—and cowered down into his magical shell. He literally shrunk away into whatever connective space the magic controlled.

I almost dropped him. Almost. But I had a grip on his aiming hand and control of his position and giving that up would give him the advantage—except his pulling back gave his shell room to work.

And to turn inside out.

CHAPTER 23

Amber magic latched onto my face. Amber glue, or sap, or the vomit of a bug flipped around from where it surrounded St. Martin and snapped itself around my head like a bubblegum bubble popping.

I gasped. Air moved into my lungs, but more slowly than it should. This wasn't the oily low-demon-like rage magic my brother had used. This was barrier magic, the kind that keeps the mundane world at bay. St. Martin—no, his genie—had distilled it into a plastic bag he'd pulled over my head.

I whipped St. Martin into the trees and clawed at the magic goo wrapped around my head. He vanished into the storm and hit a tree not too far away. The thud echoed through the hissing of the snow and ice. He groaned. I tried once again to inhale.

The amber turned the grayness of the snow into a muddy brown, and the tree trunks to black. It amplified the roaring, both of my own blood in my ears and the blizzard's winds, and what could have been a navigable woodland became a raging, watery cyclone.

I got air. My exhalation vented below the magic and around the skin of my face and out around my ears.

It had edges. I clawed at where the magic touched my hairline, looking for something to hook onto.

But the amber magic didn't so much have an end but a point at which it foamed—it would not touch my elven tattoos, but had filled in around the lines in a filigree that felt like a nest of glass under my fingers.

What was on my face? I inhaled again, and felt air pull in through those little filigree holes—and I was pretty sure Yggdrasil and my Alfheim enclave markings had just unintentionally saved my life.

St. Martin stumbled through the snow. He hunched as if the hit against the tree had done real injury, and swung his gun up once again. "My genie says you're not a real jotunn, you liar."

He fired.

A yellow and orange flash of light blossomed around the muzzle. A boom followed, one loud enough it would echo through the trees, even with the howling of the wind. And a bullet smashed into my shoulder.

Flesh parted before its force, as did my clavicle. Bone fragments erupted into the non-parted flesh as the bullet, too, fragmented.

Those fragments kept moving. Most embedded in my shoulder blade. One exited and struck my tricep.

I've been shot before. I'd fought in the Civil War. I'd had a magic pike through my chest. But this was the first time my reconstituted body had to deal with a high-velocity, modern bullet.

It wouldn't kill me. I might bleed, and I might deal with the excruciating fire of the pain it caused, but I would not die.

That is, if I could get enough air to not pass out.

I dropped to my knees.

St. Martin sneered once again, but then looked up as if he heard something my preoccupied body did not.

He tipped his head as if listening to an earpiece, nodded once, and shot another bullet into the air.

I gasped but did not fall. My blood dripped onto the swirling, pristine whiteness of the snowfall. And St. Martin grinned like the monster he was.

The amber darkened, or my brain contracted what sensory information it would process as it prioritized surviving. I couldn't tell which. I gasped again, and...

Clockwork magic lifted St. Martin off the ground. Magic that filled the gray between the snowflakes with a blinding brilliance dimmed by both the amber suffocating me and the pain ricocheting through my shoulder.

Dagrun, I thought.

The elven magic contracted. Did St. Martin drop the gun? I couldn't see. The amber stopped my attempt to inhale. Was I blacking out?

"Gee..." I tried say. "Genie..."

Dag's armor flashed as she flipped St. Martin onto his back. He landed in the snow with a thud loud enough I heard it through the amber and the roar of my own blood.

She punched a glowing fist straight into his face.

I tried to gasp. I did. I wouldn't die. I hadn't yet, and magic bug glue on my face wouldn't do it today. I'd survive...

"Frank!" Other hands touched my neck along the edges of the amber. "He shot you."

Axlam's glowing golden wolf eyes and extending canines appeared in what little I had left of my field of vision.

She growled. "What kind of magic is this? Dagrun!" she yelled.

"Sif..." I panted.

Axlam wrapped her fingers around the sides of my face and yanked. "Dagrun sent her for the other elves." The amber didn't move. She yanked once more. The magic still did not move.

Whatever Dag hit St. Martin with wasn't enough, nor had he lost his gun. He rolled to the side and fired again.

Axlam ducked. "I will string... his entrails... through the treeeees," she shouted. Her fingers curled around the edges of the amber again, but this time, her now-claw-like nails dug into my skin.

She snapped the murky amber and the chunk over half my mouth pulled off my skin as if she'd ripped off duct tape.

I gasped.

St. Martin fired again at Dag. She twisted with such speed she moved out of the way of the bullet and crossed the distance between them before he could compensate.

Dag hit him with a straight-on jab to the nose.

"Hold still," Axlam said. "You bleed." She ripped another piece of the amber off my face and fully uncovered my mouth. "Do *not* wiggle like prey, Frank Victorsson."

"He... said... he worked... for a... genie," I gasped.

Axlam whipped around. She was about to bound toward St. Martin, but I grabbed her arm.

"He wants to feed the kids... to you, Axlam," I panted. "After you... turn for the run."

She howled, but her more wolf-like traits receded. She was holding her wolf magic in check by sheer willpower.

But some of that rage remained. She raked her nails over the largest piece of amber clinging to my face. If the magic hadn't been there, she would have taken both my eyes.

The amber cracked. She swiped again, and the cold, crystalline wind blasted against my now raw skin. The amber still clung to me, but I could see. I could breathe.

I slowly stood. My head swam, and the whipping snow blurred the fight and Axlam, but I wouldn't topple over.

I bled and my shoulder had yet to stabilize or reset itself. "Stay behind me," I said. "Stay out of his magic's reach." But I could still help.

Axlam shoved me backward. "You bleed."

St. Martin rolled. Dagrun hit him with another bolt of elven magic, yet he continued to dance in and out of the increasingly thick storm. He continued to hold the gun.

The blizzard hissed like a distant plane engine, or a nearby magical serpent. It was both mundane in its power and charged with duty as a veil—this blizzard, on this approaching evening, had taken on much more meaning than *stay inside*. A lot more.

The gray of the storm was rapidly changing over to black. "How long before the moon forces you to change?" The sun, out there on the other side of the clouds, must have dropped to its low early-evening angle.

Axlam fidgeted like a fighter readying for a bout. "Soon," she said.

A sigil sliced through the whiteout. St. Martin yelped.

"Where are they?" I ripped the remaining large bits of the amber off my face. "That magic is still embedded in open areas of my tattoos." Not that I could do anything about it now. I just hoped it didn't burrow into my scalp.

A rapidly-moving, body-shaped shadow flew toward us through the snow. Axlam responded before I did, and snatched the body around the neck just as I realized it was St. Martin.

Even with Dagrun throwing him at us, he still managed to fire another shot.

Axlam didn't flinch or duck this time. She swung his body toward me. I caught his shoulder with my good arm, and flipped him over so he faced downward.

Axlam and I slammed him into the frozen ground.

His magic shell could only stop so much. His leg snapped, and likely a rib or two. He coughed. Maybe snickered.

The hit hurt him, but it didn't hurt his magic.

The gloom and the snow blurred everything now, even Axlam, who was no more than four feet to my left. But I knew exactly what the glow coming off St. Martin's carapace meant.

He was powering up just like he had in the Admin Complex parking lot.

I reached for Axlam. "He's—"

I reached, and touched blood. He'd shot her.

She gasped and staggered toward me. And I knew why the bullet in my shoulder had fragmented the way it had. Why I could feel it embed itself in my bones.

He'd shot me with silver.

"Axlam!" I pulled her close and pressed my hand over the wound on her upper arm. The bullet had ripped through her blue jacket and grazed her upper arm. "It didn't embed." Maybe she'd be okay.

"... change..." Axlam growled. She snapped. I ducked out of the way, but I knew if I didn't hold her with us, she'd bolt into the trees silver-infested under a Samhain moon, frantic about her son, and without an elf to help her hold onto her humanity.

I had to do something. "Concentrate on my voice!" I yelled. "Axlam!"

St. Martin pushed himself up. A wave moved through the magic of his carapace, then shifted upward into whining brightness obvious through the blizzard.

"Dagrun! We need to move!" I yelled. "He's about to explode!"

She manifested out of the blizzard as a goddess of ice and snow. Frost swirled around her armor-clad body. The cold had solidified as a Norse helmet over her head and face. And her elven hair, her purely magical prehensile ponytail, crackled with the power of the blizzard.

Two hundred years in Alfheim and I had never seen the full glory of an elf in battle. I'd glimpsed it when Magnus pulled me out of Vampland. I'd seen it at a distance through a drunken haze the night Rose killed herself. But this was different.

Dagrun, the Queen of the Alfheim elves, was, in this moment, the Warrior Queen of Midgard.

She moved as if dancing with the storm in order to harness the torque of its winds. The blades of magic extending from both her fists pulled in the ice swirling in the air. A new sigil formed over St. Martin's body.

She slammed her foot into the back of St. Martin's head.

But even with all her speed, and the power of her magic, she didn't see the shape of the blizzard's maw above us. Axlam, growling from the pain of the silver and the coming moon, stood rigidly at my side.

They were magicals. They probably felt the explosive bursting of St. Martin's shell as it reached upward for the descending snout, but they didn't see the teeth. They didn't see the distant magic that was, somehow, manipulating the shadows between the ice and snow.

The magic stored in St. Martin's shell exploded. And that maw, that muzzle, snapped down onto the column, us, and St. Martin.

And that muzzle pulled meat from the bone.

CHAPTER 24

I had to do something. Anything.

The blast ignited the remaining magic amber embedded around my Yggdrasil tattoo. White hot fire raged across my scalp and down my neck, and merged with the remaining pain from my still-bleeding gunshot wound.

I staggered backward, tripping over a branch or rock buried in the snow. I couldn't break my fall. Not with my damaged arm. So I was about to drop, blasted off my feet by a carrion beetle's exploding shell, and land in a way that might cause a snapped bone, or a concussion, or something worse.

Except I didn't. I tripped. I lost my balance. But my back rammed against something glass-smooth and solid. Something invisible, yet tangible.

Something amber-colored.

The hole in my shoulder throbbed with a burning rawness. Random spikes of searing agony mirrored by the heat embedded in my skin. My vision wavered—or maybe the magic did. A pulse moved through the wall and for a microsecond—for less than a blink—I saw pews.

Another searing blast of heat ignited the small spaces inside my

Yggdrasil tattoo and formed a pattern of pain along my scalp, behind my ear, and down my neck. I felt the world tree in negative relief—it soothed as the world around it burned.

I bellowed and punched the amber magic.

The wall pulsed once more—as did the magic in my tattoo—except this time, the elven magicks on my person fought back.

The World Tree would not be felled by a toad.

Around us, outside the dome of amber magic, the blizzard rumbled like a distant tornado. Ice whipped through the air and into my nostrils even as the magic held it at bay. The wind stripped heat from my skin even as the dome stopped its push.

But the World Tree cast its own protections. The pews returned as four rows of rough-hewn benches. Each looked to be its own tree, and just as much grown as it was shaped by tools. I stood off to the side with my back still against the "wall," the front of this new space to my right and the entrance to my left.

An altar grew at the front of the space, and like the door, the window behind it swirled with the icy pastels of the trapped blizzard.

The walls of the dome fluttered, and though they obscured the raging snow outside, they did not conceal, and pulsed with figures carved from the same wood as the benches: Odin. Frigg. Thor. Baldur. Freya. Frey. Heimdall. Loki. Hel. The church of Yggdrasil reached upward toward Asgard, and…

It reached outward to others. To spirits I did not recognize. Spirits of the land on which it stood. Other spirits that carried a sense of warm seas and sand, of trade and farming, of a rich world far from the Norse.

"Axlam?" I called. Was the Yggdrasil magic embedded in my scalp somehow connecting to an ancient heritage of East Africa?

She'd been hurt. Shot, just before the dome formed. She'd been standing right next to me. And Dagrun, she'd slammed her fist into St. Martin and he'd responded. He'd torqued her body.

Where were the women?

"Frank."

Axlam was right there, right next to me, seated on the end of the closest pew. She stared at her blood-covered, now-gloved hands. The wound on her shoulder had soaked her bright blue jacket and added a sudden metallic acidity to the cold scent of the snow.

"Your jacket is ruined," she said.

I also bled, and my blood had soaked the shoulder of my jacket more so than hers had her own. "I'll be fine." She was right on the edge of the pew, and like me, too close to the wall for comfort.

"Are you..." Her wolf was here, somewhere. It, like us, was trapped inside the dome, and even though it tethered to her body, it wasn't *here*.

"I am taking... measures." She scooted down the bench. "Sit, son of Victor."

Once, not long after I moved to Alfheim, I'd asked Gerard about the change. A werewolf could hold it at bay in much the same way as a person could hold a noxious smell at bay by holding their breath.

It worked, but only for a moment.

And after a while, that breath needed taking. You'd either black out, and then there'd be none of your humanity when the change came, or you could just gulp in the air and deal with the bad fumes, and the breaking bones. With the ripped skin and the popped eyeballs. With the teeth and the claws.

Axlam must have found a way stay awake while jamming a breathing tube down her own throat.

I glanced around the church. "Where's Dagrun? St. Martin?"

She pointed with her chin. "The altar."

I looked again.

Ornately carved vines both coiled and grew around the living altar while also being of the main column of wood. Leaves that were green —yet also golden, orange, and red—grew, rustled, and fell. Rain touched the crown over the altar, as did wind and snow.

The unconscious St. Martin lay facedown on the snow-covered floor. He suffered at least two fractures to his right leg. Blood pooled under his mouth and nose. He breathed, if barely.

Dagrun, her back pressed against the altar, sat with her legs out and her arms at her sides. Her armor had vanished, and she wore only the jeans and t-shirt she'd been in at my house. Yet she showed no wounds, nor had her personal magicks been disrupted.

"She still glamours." Axlam twisted enough to brush against my pocket. "Leave those plates here, Frank. Set them on the pew."

"Plates? What plates?" I saw no food.

Axlam twisted her head as if listening to someone. "They're in your pocket."

I patted along my jacket, and sure enough, I carried two daguerreotype photographic plates. One was of St. Martin close up, and the other was St. Martin and the descending wolf maw. "I don't remember finding these." Perhaps they fell out of Rose's notebook before we were attacked.

Axlam pinched her eyes closed. "My wolf makes a deal."

A deal? "Axlam…"

She shook her head. "Please, Frank."

"Okay." I pulled both plates from my pocket and set them on the wood of the pew.

"Thank you," Axlam said.

Something huge and wild brushed against my side. It pushed between us and the wall as it ran headlong into the dome between the altar and the front pew.

A howl erupted from the spirit. The dome vibrated, and for another split second, the reality of the blizzard reasserted itself. A bone-chilling gust hit my face. Shadows snapped down onto us. Axlam and I sat on the ground. Dagrun leaned against a tree with St. Martin at her feet.

Then it was gone, and we were back in Yggdrasil's church.

"The moon calls," Axlam said.

She should be changing. Dagrun should be at her side filtering the wolf's rage and offering magical support.

But she was not. "Is this your deal?" I asked. "To hold off your wolf until it is safe for you to turn?"

She nodded.

"What did you trade? Besides the plates."

"The same as you, son of Victor. A promise to help when the time comes." She gripped her arm. "Do you know what the elves do, when we run?" she asked.

I didn't go out. I wasn't privy to the magic, but I did listen to what the elves said. "Hold the feral in check," I said.

"They tell the other elves that it's their guidance that keeps our feral side under control, but that's not correct. They act as flashlights in the dark. They illuminate Alfheim so that we can clearly see our human lives." Axlam pressed her hand over the wound on her arm. "The wolf, it can consume a person. It can eat the sun and the moon and it can leave you with nothing but an eternal blackness. Nights like tonight make the wolf stronger."

Gerard and Remy once told me the same thing. That the elves illuminate the dark corners where the beast draws its power.

The power that brushed my side rammed the dome again. The magic rumbled, but held.

The power howled.

"Your wolf is trying to escape, isn't it?" I asked.

Axlam nodded. "I am the last of the pack to change. My mate's scent touches my wolf. I smell his fear and his rage. I am missing. Our cub is missing. The Elf King blazes for Gerard and holds high that bright flame to illuminate his humanity."

Could I help? I had no idea what to do.

She glanced toward the altar. "We are the only pack that runs with elves."

I knew that. They were also the largest and most stable pack in the world.

"They do help." She stared at St. Martin. "But the truth is that the politics of the run helps the elves just as much, maybe more, than they help us."

All the magicals in Alfheim understood the symbiosis of the elves and the werewolves, though like most people, I'd held the belief that the elves held a stronger position than the wolves.

"We need to get you out of here," I said. "Both you and Dagrun."

Axlam's wolf rammed the dome again. This time, she flinched.

She wasn't controlling it as well as she usually did.

"The silver has weakened my hold," she said. "I'm having an allergic reaction along with bleeding all over my coat." She looked down at the wound. "Help me with this," she said. "Rip the coat, but not too much. I still need it against the cold."

My damaged insides, though still painful, had reformed into something passible as a shoulder blade, and allowed movement. I carefully ripped her jacket, but not so much that the sleeve fell off.

She removed the pins that held her hijab in place, and pulled off the scarf. Underneath she wore a second scarf, wrapped tightly around her head.

"It's cold out, Frank," she said.

I chuckled.

Axlam grinned. "Tie it around the wound."

I wound the scarf tightly around her bicep and knotted it off just as her wolf slammed into the magic again.

"Help me stand," she said. "The silver is making me woozy."

I offered my hand. She took it, and together we exited the pew.

"The elves, like their gods, think they have all things wolf under control," Axlam muttered.

She wasn't wrong. We were all well aware of elven blind spots. I'd long believed one of the reasons Arne and Dag brought in strays was because we filled in the holes. We strays were strategic.

"He might have a revenge fantasy, but this magic," Axlam waved her good hand at the dome, "it doesn't care about me." She took a step toward the altar. "Nor did his father."

We also knocked into the pews. "Careful," I said.

"I think you and I have that in common, Frank. Suffering at the hands of entitled men of hubris."

I helped her toward Dagrun. "Aye, Axlam, this we do." Though I fully understood why her strength and resolve needed to be so much stronger than my own. I could pass as one of those men of hubris. Axlam could not.

"Legend says the first werewolf was brought to heel by a god." Axlam gripped my arm. "The wolf manifests when the moon obscures that god and unleashes the many rages of repression."

Arne did say the magicals were born of the friction of mundane against the nature of the world. Las Vegas Wolf had described some of these frictions as new ways. And here was Axlam, a woman who'd been sucked into another culture's old rage by an evil man.

But the first werewolf? The poor soul who originated the curse that Axlam, her husband, his brother, her son—all of the Alfheim Pack and every werewolf everywhere—carried? He was lost in the mists of time. Unlike the vampires who traced their origins to Vlad the Impaler, no one knew the first werewolf's name. They did, though, know that werewolves have been with mundanes since the mundanes turned wolves into dogs.

Perhaps that first werewolf wasn't a good soul. Perhaps he was. No one knew. But he did make the first Faustian deal with one of the Earth's most primal gods.

Axlam paid the price to contain that dark canine magic every time she changed.

"Gerard and Remy have always suspected a major Wolf spirit out there. One bigger and meaner than all the individual cultural manifestations. There's too much continuity between all of the variations of werewolf. We're *all* pack, unlike the elves and the fae or the kami. There are a lot of different types of werewolves, but the magic is the same."

I nodded.

"I *feel* it, Frank," she whispered. "The World Wolf. I feel its presence every day." We took another step toward Dagrun. "After Rose passed, did you ever feel her presence?" Axlam asked.

"Like a ghost?" Presences could mean all sorts of different things, when magicals were involved.

"Not a *ghost* ghost," she said. "Not like the manifestations your brother sent after you when he showed up. I mean that memory presence, the kind you get when your memory of someone, your longing and your loss, hits the parts of your mind that build your perception of the world. That injection into reality of a very real part of you is, was, will always be your mirror of the missing."

"Maybe," I said. "I think so."

"I felt that way for decades after his father bit me."

I didn't say anything. I let her speak.

"Werewolves—all of us—feel that all the time about the Wolf world-spirit. Sometimes it's small. Sometimes it takes over. Sometimes it's old school *loup-garou*. Sometimes it's a teenager in a Kenyan refugee camp." She steeled herself for another step. "That mirror, that very real part of me that is the World Wolf, is right here." She tapped her chest. "And here." She tapped her temple. "I am *pack first*, no matter who I am."

Sometimes I felt that way about the presence of my father. I mirrored Victor Frankenstein the way Axlam mirrored the World Wolf, even though we didn't mean—or want—to do so.

"That is why the elves do *not* have everything wolf under control."

No, they didn't.

"There is no room in the pack for those who steal and whine," Axlam muttered. "No place for the conniving or the manipulative. Everyone behaves or there are consequences."

We stopped within kicking distance of St. Martin.

"I fear for my son." Axlam's wolf manifested in front of the altar and directly over St. Martin as a sleek midnight-black beast. Violets and blues danced along her coat, and reds and oranges through her snarling teeth.

I'd never seen the wolf this real without a turning, yet she sniffed at St. Martin, a ten-foot-tall at the shoulders bundle of the raw rage of nature.

Dagrun and St. Martin gasped awake at exactly the same time. But Dagrun, unlike the insect with the broken leg, was our Warrior Queen.

She had one foot on St. Martin's shoulder and a hand on his forehead before he finished sucking in his breath.

He shrieked. She moved her hand so it covered his mouth, but not his nose, and looked up at Axlam's wolf. "My friend," she said. "What do you need?"

The wolf sniffed her face, and magic moved between them.

"Yes," Dagrun said. "I understand."

"Your protocols be damned, Dagrun. You need to help Ed and his family," Axlam said. "He is the town monster slayer. He is not a mundane who will hurt you."

She was talking as if she wasn't going to make it out of this alive.

Dag pinched her lips.

"I will get you to the pack," I said. "I promise."

Axlam touched my chest. "Thank you."

A new bolt of amber magic blasted from St. Martin's eyes, ears, and mouth. It coiled out of his nose. And it pushed Dagrun away.

He rolled onto his side. "Look at the puppy!" He wheezed. "You open my magicks, and she's going to rampage, aren't you, darling? Your mate is frantic out there in the snow, isn't he? You exit my trap and all that dark wolf power is going to do exactly what my genie said it would! You'll kill an elf or two. Maybe go into town and kill that annoying sheriff. You'll do exactly what—"

Dagrun slammed a hand over his mouth again, and lifted her free hand. Her fingers moved, and a sigil formed. "Frank," she said. "You two need to leave now, while I can manipulate the magic."

She wasn't coming.

Dagrun moved so that she straddled St. Martin's chest. "I can't open the dome, but I can force it to allow you to leave. Do you understand?"

Axlam touched my arm. "We will still be inside, but not at this location."

Dag nodded. "Get her to the pack, Frank. Find my husband. The shell must be ripped open."

"What about you?" I asked.

Dag pressed down on St. Martin's face. "I am sorry, Axlam. I'm sorry I allowed this to happen. I'm sorry this magic hid its true nature."

Axlam closed her eyes. "Can you get Frank outside the magic?"

Dag shook her head. "No."

"Frank." Axlam gripped my hand. "You are inside the shell with me. When I change, you won't be able to get away. Don't let me hurt you."

I wouldn't hurt her. Not to save myself.

Axlam wiped at her eye. "Damn it, Frank." She gave me a quick side-hug.

"You need to be Axlam's elf until you find the pack," Dag said. "Talk to her. Keep her awake, do you understand? Her wolf *will* overwhelm everything we've done to hold it off. You must keep her awake so *she* turns and not the rage."

"I will," I said to Dag, then to Axlam, "I *will*."

She nodded.

"Go," Dag said, and flashed her sigil against the side of my head.

The piercing white-hot agony between my tattoo's branches returned. It lifted off my skin as if drawn into the ice and snow of the blizzard and floated for a moment above St. Martin as a negative space relief of the magic that, right now, mitigated the worst of his amber shell.

He stopped struggling.

Axlam's wolf pushed her snout into his face. "You came here because you wanted to see yourself as the tamer of the Wolf. That's why you keep on about civility and management," Axlam's beast said-growled. "You want me on the ground begging. You want me to relive your father's death to show your dominance because you're perpetually terrified of your own shadow. You're just another weak, twisted mind doing someone else's evil."

He yelled once again against Dagrun's hand.

"You will never understand how pathetic you are."

"Frank!" Dagrun said. "Remember! Keep her awake." Then the Queen of the Elves hit the dome with the fragmented relief of my scalp's Yggdrasil.

CHAPTER 25

Cold wind raked across my face. Ice stuck in my ears, and snow to my eyelashes. The blizzard hid everything—trees, the ground, the sky—behind a veil of gunmetal gray.

"Axlam," I shouted. She had been right next to me. Dagrun and St. Martin had been in front of us no more than five feet away.

But I could barely see my own hand in front of my face.

"Dagrun!" I stumbled forward—and into Axlam. She was on the ground, on all fours. She panted and growled, and couldn't be more than minutes from turning.

"I'll get you to the pack. I'll get you to Arne. He'll get the silver out of your arm. You'll be okay."

The wound wasn't tied. She still wore her scarf and her hands were bare again and showing signs of turning into claws.

She was also located where, when we were inside the dome, her wolf had been standing over St. Martin. But he wasn't here, and neither was Dagrun.

"Axlam," I touched her back. "Stand up. Please. Dag wanted me to get you to the pack."

She sat back on her heels. "Mate," she snarled.

Her eyes were fully wolf-like, and a hint of a muzzle pushed out around her nose and mouth.

Axlam howled, and the wind howled right along with her. A gust hit us, but her howl didn't travel with it. It reverberated inside the shell we still carried.

I sucked in my breath as the vibration set my teeth on edge.

Axlam yipped and covered her ears. "Hold it hold it hold it," she said.

I only wore my jacket. No gloves, no hat. I'd be fine, but Axlam in her human form would not. "Can you walk?" She'd said the silver was causing an allergic reaction and throwing off her balance.

She snarled again, and shook her head. "Where... cub?"

"I don't know." St. Martin hadn't taken the kids. That was clear. And he had no knowledge of his boss taking them, either.

But the "genie" could have still taken Jax and the girls.

I swung Axlam up into my arms. "Can you get a scent through the shell? Do you smell Dagrun? The pack?"

She stiffened as if holding her wolf back hurt worse than the gunshot wound. I had no doubt that it did. "Dag is..." she growled. "I will... hurt you... if change..."

"Then hold it," I said. "Which way should I go to get you to the pack?"

Dagrun could take care of herself. Axlam needed to be my main worry at the moment.

She pressed her bleeding arm against my chest. "My... brother... by another... messed up... father..." she said.

It must be bad if she was making jokes. "Which way, Alpha of the Alfheim Pack?"

She sniffed. "West."

The storm swirled around us. My face had already lost most of my heat, and the cold bit into my ears and cheeks. Snow hit my eyes and I couldn't make out any landmarks. "Which way is west?"

She weakly pointed over my shoulder.

"How long can you hold the turn?" I doubted I could carry a

changing werewolf, and if I set her down, she'd bolt into the trees wild on rage, Samhain, and silver poisoning.

She coughed.

"Talk to me." I stumbled through the snow. "Maybe we should sing a song."

Axlam coughed again. "Tell me... about... your seer."

She remembered Ellie? "Her name is Ellie Jones," I said. "I don't remember much more than that. She has a friend in Tokyo. Her name is Chihiro. The two kitsune in Vegas connected us. I've been able to track what I can because of Chihiro."

I'd made a deal with those two kitsune.

Axlam sniffed. "You... love her."

"Is it that obvious?" I almost tripped over a log, but I got us through.

"Samhain loosens..." She cough-growled again, and shivered in my arms.

"If you turn, promise me you won't get mad if I sit on you." Maybe she'd hold onto her humanity long enough to *not* rip up the world —and me.

Axlam cough-chuckled. "There's a song..." she said, "... Thirty-eight Special.... 'Hold on Loosely'... Gerard loves that song..."

And here I never took Gerard as an eighties-arena-rock kind of guy.

"We were in the car... on the way back from Fargo... college... came on radio...." She stiffened and growled again. "He sang along with the... radio..."

Was I just treated to the Alfheim Pack's alpha mate meet-cute story? But it made sense. Axlam wanted to hold onto her joy.

Her shivers picked up speed and intensity. "Come to our house... I will teach you to make... sambusas."

"Sambusas?" I asked.

"Better than... lefse."

"Oh, now, them's fightin' words." I swung her between two trees. "Maybe we should yell that into the storm. Nothing brings elves faster than disrespecting their favorite potato-based food."

She coughed.

I took us around a big tree. One I thought I recognized. "Axlam? I think we're near my lake." The snow grayed out everything, and without the moon visible, the world was shadows and ice.

"If I change now... I'll kill you..."

The blizzard howled. How were the wolves and the elves running in this? "No, you will not. I'm already dead, remember?"

Axlam snarled.

Her hand on my shoulder elongated. She dug her nails into my shoulder.

I stopped running. The snow caked the side of my face, and coated Axlam's jacket and scarf. We were unintentionally camouflaged into the raging ice around us.

"Axlam?"

She spasmed. Her back arched. The moon, behind the ceiling of gusts and gray, must have been fully out.

Whatever the deal was—whatever she'd sacrificed to get the few minutes we had away from the dome running toward the lake—popped like a balloon. I did not see it leave her body, but I felt it fly as if the storm was lifting a bird into its toothsome jaw.

I had no idea how to help. She would get away from me sooner or later—no matter how strong and fast I might be, she was a werewolf and capable of inflicting enough damage to take me down.

I hadn't been fast enough. I hadn't gotten her up the hill and to the lake, where the pack would find her. I'd let her down.

I set her on a log. "What should I do?" Should I help with her clothes? But the boots and the pants and the coat might slow her down enough that I could restrain her until the pack arrived.

Her hands and face elongated, and she rolled onto all fours.

I stepped back. There wasn't any more I could do. "I'm so sorry." Would she burn out the silver fast enough to come back to herself?

Axlam lifted her face to the storm above and howled. The magic reverberated again, and we both cringed. But the cry erupted from her throat with such force it pierced the snow. It pierced the wind and the ice. It rose above.

And there, off to the south, a faint answer.

I dropped to my knees. "Someone heard your howl. They're coming."

Ice coated my head and face. Snow collected in the folds of Axlam's scarf. But the wind carried her howls.

Axlam reared up onto her legs. "Jaxssssoooonnn!" she howled.

The kids…. They'd vanished. We'd felt St. Martin's approach and the girls had… I couldn't remember. They'd been next to the gate telling us about the spell Akeyla had set over my dog's water, and then they'd disappeared.

My axe called from somewhere nearby.

"Sal!" I yelled. "We're over here!"

CHAPTER 26

J axson found us first. He burst through the gloom in full wolf
form, a violet-black bundle of magic trailing waves and waves of
frantic energy. He ran right by me and to his mother's side.

Sal called out to me again.

"Over here!" I yelled.

Out in the snow, no more than twenty feet away, the magic of her
blade lit up like a beacon.

"Hold on, Axlam," I said.

"Uncle Frank!" Akeyla yelled. She burst through the storm just as
Jaxon had, a little elf with a glowing axe as big as she was on her
shoulder. A bubble of her warm fire magic kept the snow and cold off
not only her, but also off Sophia, whose hand she held.

"We're here, Mrs. Geroux." Akeyla set Sal on the ground next to
Axlam and expanded the bubble to include all of us.

"Where have you kids been?" I asked. "Akeyla, stay back. Axlam is
changing, honey."

Akeyla pinched her lips together. "Jax says I can help." She put her
hands on Axlam's cheeks. "There's something here. It feels sticky." She
lifted her hands away from Axlam's skin.

My niece blinked. She looked up at Jax, then nodded. "Okay."

She cupped Axlam's cheeks again.

Sophia took my hand. "It's okay, Mr. Frank. We know what to do."

I looked down at the little girl who carried herself so much like her father. "How?" I asked.

She watched Akeyla work. "The lady Akeyla can't see told us there was bad magic. She told me to tell Akeyla to give Ms. Geroux her light. She said if it was bright enough, it could get through the bad magic. Sal helps. The lady said she'd realized what the bad magic was and came back to tell you but she needed to hide us from the monster first." She tugged on my fingers. "She was really scared, Mr. Frank. She said none of us would remember her when she vanished. Akeyla couldn't see her anyway, and I know Jax doesn't remember, but I do."

A magical woman—a seer—protected the kids?

Sophia squeezed my hand. "Her name was Ellie. She said she was your friend."

Ellie. Ellie Jones. "Yes, she's my friend," I said. I'd forgotten about her. *Again.*

Sophia pointed at Akeyla and Sal. "She told us to use Sal to call for help after she vanished, so we did."

Axlam calmed some, under Akeyla's fingers.

Part of me wanted to scoop them all up and get them away from the changing werewolf. But another, stronger part understood that right now, my nine-year-old niece and her friends were keeping Axlam sane.

"When your friend disappeared," Sophia pointed over her shoulder, "he showed up."

I sensed him first, as if his magic tapped me on the shoulder then ran away like a kid playing ding-dong-ditch-it.

I instinctively moved Sophia behind me as I turned around.

The elf standing close enough to touch extended his hand. He was as big as Arne, and carried his shoulders the same way. He wore elven hunting leathers as black as Lennart's, as if he, too, had gone out on the run with the wolves. Elven tattoos shimmered around the naked part of his scalp, over his face, and down his neck. His ungloved hands were also covered in elven tattoos, as if someone had put wards on his skin to throw off some evil's scent.

But he was unlike any other elf I had ever met.

Never in my two hundred years had I come across an elf with gray hair and black eyes, nor had I met one who grinned like Loki himself.

"Hrokr Arnesson," he said. "I am *so* pleased to finally meet you, Frank Victorsson. We're neighbors!" He winked. "Though my father doesn't approve of the town bothering me."

He pulled back his hand when I didn't shake. "It is Samhain." He shrugged, then leaned close as if to tell me his deepest secret. "Concealment enchantments thin this time of year, my dear."

This elf lived behind concealment enchantments? "Who are you?" I asked.

He held up his hand. "One second," he said, then cocked his head as if listening.

Axlam's back arched again.

"Mr. Hrokr!" Akeyla said. "We need to call Mommy and Grandpa!"

A burst of warmth rolled by. Not Akeyla's warmth, or anything that felt particularly elven, but it did feel alive. And deep down I knew what that meant.

The shell had burst.

The elf nodded approvingly. "It is done."

Dagrun must have figured out how to break St Martin's magic.

"Jaxson, my boy," the elf said, "it's now safe to release your best howl! Your father is close. Let him know where you are."

Jaxson obliged.

"And you, my sweet girl, call in the cavalry."

Akeyla touched my axe. "Now, Sal!" she said.

A new burst of magic rolled off Sal and into the storm.

Out in the snow, several close-by wolves howled their responses. Yells followed. And out in the gray between the snowflakes, magic lit the way.

Hrokr leaned close again. "My father thinks I'm a bit... odd." He shrugged. "We are all different aspects of our magic, yes?" He pointed at the children. "When Salvation called out, I answered. It is my sacred duty to protect the children and the disadvantaged, including the other fae-born of our town."

He twisted slightly as if looking at rips and tears in my jacket, then nodded as if satisfied for some unseen reason. "I helped the kids listen, and I made sure they didn't get lost in the storm. We didn't need frozen kiddos tonight, now did we?"

"The pack's coming," Akeyla said to Axlam. "They're almost here." She touched Jaxson's snout. "Your daddy's coming."

"And then there's you." Hrokr gripped my arms and a purplish-red magic washed from his hands to my body. "Funny how you have already died and come back to us here in Midgard. So presumptuous. I like it!"

"What does that mean?" I asked. "Who *are* you?" I asked again.

He poked my chest. "Hrokr, silly. I'm a jotunn, just like you." He waved his hand and a streak of reddish magic erupted in front of us like a waterfall of fireworks.

I was a reconstituted man. He was an elf, even with the strange hair and eyes. Neither of us were real jotunn.

Akeyla looked up. "Where's Uncle Frank?" she said.

The red magic must have hidden me.

Sophia squeezed my hand again, though, and looked up at Hrokr, who touched his finger to his lips.

"If I don't hide him, he'll lose his only chance to find his friend," Hrokr said.

Sophia nodded knowingly. "Then you should go, Mr. Frank. Ellie must be worried. Please tell her we did as she asked and now everyone is safe."

Sophia seemed so certain of her words.

Then Sophia called out to Akeyla, "Mr. Frank's going to find Marcus Aurelius." She looked up at me and grinned. "It's not really a lie, is it?"

I'd long suspected someone was caring for my wayward hound. "No," I said. That someone must be Ellie Jones. "No, it's not."

Hrokr bent down and looked Sophia in the eyes. "Thank you for remembering me, my dear. I owe you a boon."

She gave him a quick hug.

"Now, do you remember what I told you to tell the first elf who comes?" he asked.

She thought for a second. "I see the truth," she said.

"Yes! Yes. Good." Hrokr straightened again to speak to me. "If my father has another of his conniptions about mundanes, it's not *prophecy*. Alfheim already has her seer." He winked at me. "It's *truth*."

The kids were not acting as if this strange elf was a danger. Perhaps he wasn't. But any elf I didn't know who called me neighbor set off all my alarms.

Hrokr gripped my elbows this time. "Time to go, darling! The evening reset has already happened, that's why you don't understand all this, but her concealments haven't closed yet." He looked at his wrist as if he wore a watch. "You have... twenty minutes? Maybe thirty before that cottage of hers shutters for the night."

"I can get through Ellie's enchantments if I go now?" I asked.

Hrokr touched his finger to the tip of his nose, then pointed the finger at me.

"Which way?" I glanced out at the blizzard raging outside Akeyla's bubble of magic. "Why are you helping me?"

"I told you already." He turned me in the direction I suspected was perpendicular to the lake. "Off you go, young man. The kids are alright. They have this."

A massive, dire-wolf-like adult werewolf leaped out the trees and into Akeyla's bubble of warmth. He shook and immediately pressed his snout against Axlam's cheek.

"Gerard!" I said.

Hrokr leaned close again. "He can't see or hear you."

Sif appeared next. She immediately ran to the kids.

Two more werewolves arrived, along with Arne and Bjorn, who immediately augmented Akeyla's bubble and wove a spell to draw the silver out of Axlam's bicep.

Hrokr Arnesson tugged on my arm. "This way."

Lennart and his wolf appeared next. He scooped up Akeyla, now with Sal on her shoulder, and took Sophia's hand to lead them away from Arne and Bjorn, who, like elven paramedics, were spinning intricate healing spells around Axlam.

Three more wolves arrived and formed a circle around Axlam and Gerard. The other elves formed their own circle farther out, a levy really, and waited.

Maura appeared, as did Benta and the remaining elder elves. Lennart handed off Akeyla, who stood with the circle. He leaned down to listen to Sophia's words, then nodded and turned his back to the circle. His hand moved and…

Ed, flashlight in hand and fully bundled in winter gear, walked through the spaces between the blowing snowflakes.

"Daddy!" Sophia shouted.

He gasped and dropped to his knees to hug his daughter. Lennart touched his shoulder. They spoke, but I couldn't hear, though I knew what he said. Lennart pulled Ed into the circle with his daughter.

"Well, look at that!" Hrokr said. "Dad's gonna be pissed." He slapped my shoulder. "Still, there might be hope for us elves yet, huh?"

"Is Axlam okay?" I asked.

He gave me another shove. "All is well in Alfheim! Go on! The window closes."

They did seem to have everything under control. "Thank you."

He extended his hand again. This time, I shook.

"Remember what I said." He vanished into the thickening snow.

A new gale blotted out what I could see of the wolves and the pack, and I turned in the direction the strange elf with the gray hair and black eyes had pointed. He'd said I had twenty minutes, thirty tops, to find my way to Ellie's cottage.

I had vague memories of notes telling me I needed to get inside her concealments, otherwise I'd never remember her. I also had vague memories that I really didn't know what Ellie Jones wanted.

I trudged forward anyway, taking the scouring blizzard wind and now-blinding snow directly in the face.

A wolf ran by so quickly its brown and white fur blended into the storm's gray. The snow roared, and the wolf moved through the cold as if what raged around us was nothing at all.

Another dire-wolf-sized beast followed. He slowed for a moment and sniffed the air, then howled for his pack to follow.

A sleek black wolf appeared. She stopped, but she did not howl. A second massive wolf padded up to her side. He sniffed at her ear and nuzzled her neck. A third smaller, black wolf trailing brilliant violet-blue magic pushed between the two larger wolves' legs.

Bjorn, Sif, and Benta appeared, one on each side of the family, both casting beacons into the cold night.

More of the pack ran by, with more elves. Gerard howled, and Remy, now off in the distance, responded.

The magicals of Alfheim disappeared behind a wall of snow.

They were okay. They would finish the run unmolested.

I returned to trekking though the blizzard, looking for a woman I did not remember. A woman who, like Axlam's World Wolf, was always there, always nearby, always touching me somehow.

Ellie Jones, the phantom around whom I built my perception of the world.

I saw no trees. I sensed no logs, or forest, or the lake. Only the wind and the ice. Only the gunmetal shadows and the sting of the cold. Had I gotten turned around? I closed my eyes against the ice onslaught. The wolves howled. The blizzard roared. And I stood alone against the storm.

A dog barked.

I opened my eyes. "Marcus Aurelius?" I called. "Here, boy!"

He barked again as if commanding the veil of the storm to part, and trotted up to my legs.

Like me, he was coated in snow and ice, and also like me, it didn't seem to bother him all that much. He shook, and snow released from his curly fur only to build up again immediately.

He jumped up to give me hound kisses.

"Where have you been?" I asked. "Can you show me the way?"

My dog turned slightly to the right of the direction I had been walking. He looked over his shoulder and barked again.

"I'm coming," I said.

He moved quickly, but I managed to keep him in sight until he passed through a creaking gate that appeared out of the storm as if it, too, had been called. A low fence of rough wood spread to the left and the right, with both sides vanishing into the storm. The gate wasn't any taller than my waist, and had been tied to the side so it didn't close. It groaned and banged on the fence, but the rope holding it in place held.

I touched the fence. It seemed the correct thing to do, to show this place some reverence. "Hello," I said, as if the cottage would talk to me the same way as Sal. But no one responded, so I stepped through.

It still snowed on the other side, but the wind diminished. To my left, a gigantic tree towered into the storm above. In the shadows between the trunk and the fence, a small herd of whitetail deer huddled—a few does, two or three yearlings, and the biggest buck I'd ever seen, with a good fifteen-point set of antlers. He snorted at my dog but continued to shelter in place.

The tree's branches were full of critters—squirrels, songbirds, and up high, I could just make out a bald eagle.

To my right, in a small courtyard filled with a woodpile, sat a doghouse, a frozen pond, an old hand-operated water pump, and several other snow-covered objects. A raccoon family watched me from inside the doghouse, and a fox huddled behind the woodpile.

None of the animals seemed too concerned about me, or my dog. They knew they were safe here, with the tree and the seer.

Her name was Ellie Jones. Marcus Aurelius had found her first, and had led her to my lake because that water pump hadn't worked. She'd needed to wash one of her photos.

I'd taken her to Lara's, and I'd gotten her the first phone.

She liked muffins.

And she'd saved me from Dracula.

Then I'd done something dumb. Ellie had cried. She'd left her bike. And she'd kissed me.

She'd kissed me at Bjorn's church, too.

"Ellie," I whispered.

Marcus Aurelius looked over his shoulder again, then back at the cottage in front of both of us. Candlelight glowed in the window off to the side of the wooden door.

Marcus Aurelius ran up to the door. He pawed. He barked.

The door opened.

"There you are!" She wore only a nightgown and socks, and the candlelight behind her backlit her shape. She hugged my cold, wet dog. "I was so worried." She sounded as if she was about to cry. "Did you find the kids? Are they okay?"

Marcus Aurelius backed away from her. He turned toward me, and barked again.

She looked up and shaded her eyes.

He ran back into the courtyard.

"Marcus Aurelius! Come!" she called. "The cottage is about to close up for the night."

She stepped out into the snow.

"Ellie." I was still by the tree, still in the shadows with the critters and out of the shaft of light flowing out of her door.

She touched her open lips. "Frank?" she called.

I stepped into the light. "There was an elf. The kids..." Why was I at a loss for words? "They're okay, Ellie. They found us. Axlam's okay. The elf said St. Martin's gone and that I should come this way and..."

"Frank!" Ellie ran into the snow in her stocking feet and her night-gown. She pressed through the wind and the ice. And Ellie jumped into my snow-covered, near-frozen arms. "Oh, Frank."

"I'm as cold as the blizzard," I said, but I held on anyway. "You'll freeze." The cottage sheltered us from the worst of the storm, but the air—and my body—were still freezing cold.

"I don't care. I don't. I don't care." She kissed me like she had at the church—as if she believed our time together would go away all too soon. She hiccupped, and tears touched my cold neck. "You're here," she whispered.

Somewhere, in the grand tree, a sweet, small bell *tinkled*.

Ellie looked up. "The cottage is about to close."

Marcus Aurelius, backlit by the candles, waited patiently just inside the door. That cottage sheltered my dog. The tree sheltered the life of the forest. And right now, the beautiful, shivering woman in my arms needed sheltering, too.

Like me, she'd been too long unmoored in her own storm.

"I remember everything," I said.

Her hiccups turned to sobs. "Come inside," she said. "Please."

She wanted me with her. She wanted me to stay.

I pulled her tightly to my cold body and did the best I could to offer the shelter she needed—I carried the woman I loved toward her own blizzard of magic.

EPILOGUE

Dagrun Tyrsdottir leaned against the altar fashioned from both living and dead ash. Like Frank, the altar was more alive than dead, though it did have a root or two still in Hel's domain.

Some things neither the World Tree nor her adopted son could avoid.

Her wrist, the one broken by Frank's unholy "brother," had fractured again, and throbbed under a layer of healing magic that was, at the moment, not doing its job.

There was a corruption here, one strong enough to trigger something in Frank. Something that she'd sensed as she'd been fighting the insect St. Martin's magic. Her adopted son had subconsciously called out into the Realms—all the Realms, not just those accessible by Alfheim's elves—for reinforcements.

Should she blame Salvation for training Frank's mind for such calls? Or perhaps this was the sensitivity she and Arne had always felt in him. The second one, beyond his synesthetic ability to see magic.

He was not mundane, this they knew. Nor was he a jotunn. The jotnar were not the giants so claimed by the faulty readings of the ancient texts done by myopic mundanes. Nor were they like the elves. They were neither good nor evil, but they gave the gods pause.

Frank was something new.

She did her best to hold her wrist in such a way as to keep the sharp bursts of pain to a minimum. St. Martin's magic had snatched her around the waist as well, and she was sure she had some sort of internal damage, and perhaps a broken rib or two.

He still breathed. Barely, but she had not yet opened his path to his chosen Land of the Dead.

She'd broken his leg in three places, and lacerated multiple internal organs. Several of her hits had been hard enough to cause skull fractures.

He had chosen of his own free will to be the avatar of a dark magic she had no choice but to contain. Not just for her friend's safety, or the safety of her town. She had taken those hits for the world.

She would again. And again. If needed she would die trying to contain this magic, as her god aspect had so many times before.

The blizzard roared beyond the illusion of Frank's sacred World Tree space, but the flutter of wings momentarily rose above the din. The air distorted as if the fluttering beats modeled the cold like clay, and the smaller of Lennart's ravens appeared directly over St. Martin's unconscious body. The bird flapped her darkly iridescent feathers and landed gently on Dagrun's thigh.

"I'd pet you," she said, "but that hand is damaged, and twisting would not be comfortable."

The raven clucked and honked. It moved closer to her face in an attempt to read her expression, then hopped off her leg to gaze at St. Martin.

The bird looked over her shoulder as if asking why he still lived.

Dag shrugged, which she should not have done, but she held the wince so as not to show the bird her pain. "He is a mundane. We have laws."

Now the bird shrugged.

"He'll be dead soon enough," Dag said.

More flutters, and the second raven appeared. It hopped onto her shoulder instead of her thigh, and picked at the altar.

"You shouldn't do that," she said.

The bigger raven rubbed its head against her hair.

"I apologize for not visiting you more," she said to the birds. "You were making friends with Lennart."

The two birds honked. Dagrun closed her eyes. Without Frank, the blizzard's deep freeze inched ever closer, and a chill crept into her bones.

The flutters happened again.

The woman now squatting on the other side of St. Martin wore black jeans and thick leather boots. Her white t-shirt all but gleamed under the golden light of Frank's magical bubble, and her leather biker jacket looked both well-worn yet new and shiny.

She adjusted the black knit cap she wore over her two long, low braids.

The World Raven ran her finger across the illusionary floor next to St. Martin's shoulder. She peered at her fingertip, frowned, then wiped her hand on his chest. "Dagrun, daughter of Tyr," she said, as she examined her fingertip again. "Living life to the fullest, I see." Another wipe, and she seemed satisfied.

"Always," Dag responded. Tricksters were not evil per se; they were, though, demanding in their expectations of their targets, and Dag had best be careful with her choice of words.

Raven leaned over St. Martin. "Did he honestly think he was dealing with a genie?"

"Evidence points to yes," Dag said. The idiotic fool.

Raven poked his shoulder. "You are one dumbass moron, you know that?"

St. Martin groaned.

Raven nodded toward Dag. "Your ex is a bag of dicks, by the way."

Dag would have shrugged again but her long-ex Niklas der Nord wasn't worth the pain. "On this we agree."

Raven stood and her jacket rustled in much the same way as the birds' feathers. "I can curse Nikky-boy, if you'd like. Something fun, like permanent jock itch. I'd do it for free just for the entertainment value."

Dagrun laugh-coughed. "He's been exiled." So no matter how

tempting Raven's offer, he would no longer be a thorn in Alfheim's side.

Raven kicked at some illusionary leaf litter. "Your friend," she looked back toward Dag, "Axlam, correct? Now there's some strong magic." She pointed to accent her assertion. "Her soul cries out against her isolation."

Dag leaned against the altar again, and didn't respond. What should she say? The universality of Axlam's pain could never be touched through its individual armor, so Dag offered what she could —her magic at runs, and her support as a friend.

Raven did not seem to agree. "That's what happens when your roots are torn out and then hacked to pieces by some random colonizer."

One should never argue with a trickster, especially a trickster stating the obvious. "You speak truth, Raven." But that's what war did, and elven magic could only do so much in response.

The two birds clucked and hopped to St. Martin to take over Raven's carrion picking duties. She watched them rub beaks and coo at each other, then rubbed her own nose. "Do you know why I am here, Empress Dagrun?"

She was not Empress. That title was held by her stepmother. Dag had her own role in this universe.

A new, menacing grin slowly appeared on Raven's lips. "Perhaps Frank should have named his dog after you instead of that long-dead Roman guy." Her words held a bit of whimsy, and for a second, Dag wondered if some part of Raven had known the real Marcus Aurelius.

"You are a feathered bundle of contradictions, World Raven," Dag said.

The grin turned to a smile, which quickly vanished. "Others heeded Frank's call." She looked around. "That isolation we spoke of has consequences." She closed her eyes and inhaled deeply. "But mostly, I enjoy interfering more than the other spirits. Ah!" She pointed at the pews and snapped her fingers.

Two photographic plates appeared in her hands. She quickly

unsleeved one, looked at it, then pushed it back into its sleeve. She did the same for the second. "Well, look at that."

Dag did not dare ask. Showing interest only egged on a trickster and gave them the upper hand, and she was too tired to play a more complicated game.

Her wrist screamed, and her other wound, the one she pressed on with all her glamouring might, was beginning to make itself felt.

"These two," Raven waved the plates at the two birds, "have decided to accept the names Huginn and Muninn, at least for the time being, as a tribute to your... injury."

Raven knew the truth behind Dag's glamour. She still wasn't about to drop it, though. Not in front of the still-breathing St. Martin. "Thank you," she said to the two birds.

They preened and clucked at Dag the way they would to a chick.

"Now you and I make a deal," Raven said.

The moment of truth. No trickster would appear to an elder elf unless he or she wished a boon.

Raven kicked St. Martin. "Wake up, dumbass."

He moaned. She kicked him again, and Huginn and Muninn returned to resting on Dag's thighs.

St. Martin groaned. He tried to move, but screamed when he realized his leg wasn't much of a leg anymore.

Raven tucked the plates into her pocket as she squatted next to his head. "Would you like me to save you? You and I can make a deal, little Renfield."

He stared up at her wide-eyed.

"That's right, you pathetic pile of dung. I'm the real deal." Raven flicked the tip of his nose.

"The genie said—"

Raven sat back on her heels. "Genie! You cannot seriously be that stupid."

"But..." St. Martin visibly tensed. His rage was cresting over his pain.

"Here's the thing, ugly weasel boy—you are, as the kids say these days, *the worst*." She flicked his nose again. "You come rolling into town all wrapped up in your petty rage over a slight on your French honor." Raven slapped St. Martin. "Your 'genie' sent you here to test the magical waters of Alfheim, you moron. He doesn't care if you drown."

He wheezed out words Dag could not make out.

"What's that? Not feeling so well? Did Dagrun the Wanderer kick the living mediocrity out of your pathetic ass? Poor boy."

That "genie's" magic had kicked Dagrun in the face. And the gut. She pulled her magicks tighter, to hold her wrist together.

And just about every place else.

Raven squeezed St. Martin's chin. "You were incidental. Your target, as such targets usually are, is just a woman trying to live her life."

"She killed my—"

Raven slapped him so hard his opposite cheek slammed against the ground. "Shut up."

He groaned again and fell silent.

"I could force you into a servitude not unlike the purpose you serve right now, but I think you'd like it too much." Raven rolled her eyes. "Or I could ignore you and concentrate on the bigger picture."

She stood and wiped her hands on her pants as if slapping him had left slime on her palms. Gingerly, she stepped over his body.

She sat cross-legged next to Dagrun. "His so-called genie did you grave injury, Dagrun Gallows' Burden."

Dag leaned against the altar again. "I will heal."

Raven elbowed her gently. "I bet you always say that."

She did. "Good times, huh?" If good times meant wounds and watching mundanes die.

St. Martin's head lolled to the side, and his breathing became erratic. He was about to expire.

"I don't have the magic to save him," Dag said.

Raven sniffed. She did, she just didn't want to. Dag had no desire to argue about it.

One last exhale, and he stilled.

The pews vanished, as did the door and the church window, but the altar stayed. St. Martin's corpse cooled in the snow, but the World Tree continued to shelter Dag and the trickster world spirit.

Raven pulled the two plates from her pocket. "Your friend traded the proof these plates hold for the extra strength she needed to make it to her pack."

This, Dagrun knew. She'd sensed Axlam making the deal. There'd been something with Frank, as well. Something she could not remember.

Raven smoothed her hand over one of the sleeves. "Your friend made it, by the way."

Dagrun exhaled for what felt like the first time since St. Martin's attack. "Thank all the gods."

Her husband would find her the moment she sent away the trickster. She could go home. Rest. And figure out the best way to move forward. "What do you want?"

Raven clucked, and Huginn and Muninn took up pecking at St. Martin's now-blue corpse. "I want what is mine by name."

She wanted Raven's Gaze. Dag shook her head. "The pub belongs to Bjorn Thorsson. It is not mine to give."

Raven laughed.

Dag frowned.

The sly grin on Raven's lips meant only one thing—she thought she had already won. "Your husband will find you shortly." She leaned closer. "I like him more than your ex. He lives up to that whole aspect thing. Plus he's one fine man." Raven touched her ear. "It's the notches. They're battle-scar sexy."

"I'm glad you approve," Dag said.

Raven fiddled with the plates. "Frank told you about Las Vegas Wolf and his dire-pups." Her words were not a question, but a statement.

"Yes," Dag said.

"You know of the World Wolf. All wolves feel it, the World Wolf."

"Yes."

Raven pulled one of the plates from its sleeve. "There is a wolf," she said. "One that is rage and hunger. One that, if it breaks its chains, will come for the world."

The same wolf whose presence she'd felt in St. Martin's "genie" magic.

"It is good to know that we are on the same page," Raven said.

Dag slowly exhaled. "Why do you care, Raven?" She was too tired to be polite, and the altar had begun to fade. The blizzard's chill touched her wounds and only added to the throbbing.

Raven straightened her knit hat. "Because the rest of the world is sick of suffering the side effects inflicted by your one worst wolf."

Each time that wolf broke his bonds, the elves and their mundanes did not suffer side effects. They died.

Dag slowly took the plate with her non-damaged hand. The seer had gotten enough distance on St. Martin to reveal the full size and extent of the magic he channeled—and the shape of its source.

She hadn't realized until St. Martin pulled Frank, Axlam, and her inside his shell. She'd thought it just another strong Wolf, like Las Vegas Wolf, who had found a way to smear out its magic.

She'd never been so wrong in her life.

"Fenrir," she said.

"All you need to do is ask for help," Raven responded.

The World Raven sitting next to Dagrun was a trickster, but she was also the trickster who brought light to the world.

"You'll help stop Ragnarok in exchange for a restaurant?"

Raven smugly examined her fingernails. "Plus a few other things."

Of course there would be "other things."

"It's not much. Just a spark or two."

The World Raven wanted an elven *spark*.

"Don't look so crestfallen, Odinsdottir."

Raven wanted a babe. "Don't call me that. Two Odin aspects cannot govern an enclave. It's forbidden." Dag refused to answer Raven's other proclamation.

Raven bit one of her examined nails. "Dagrun Delight of Frigg."

Dag ignored the bait.

"Oh! Dagrun Eagle Head. No, wait, best not to annoy the World Eagle."

"My name is Dagrun Tyrsdottir." She fully dropped her glamour, hoping to put a stop to the names.

Raven made a faux-disgusted face. "You should probably fix that."

"Why should I? I see fine." If she revealed her true lack-of-eye to the world, she might need to wear a patch, and no one wanted a one-eyed queen.

Raven clasped her shoulder. "Aye, you do, my friend."

Magic burst between the whipping snowflakes. "Dagrun!" Arne's frantic voice called out from the storm. He'd find her momentarily, and then they'd find their way home.

Raven dusted the snow off her shoulders. "It's a shame Ragnarok's gonna kill that fine man of yours."

Behind Dag, the altar fully dissipated. She no longer had its support. She no longer had anything between her and the raging gray flatness of a world without a sun or a moon. "No," she said. Nothing else. Nothing more. Only her refusal to allow the inevitable to happen.

She would keep her husband safe.

Raven whistled. "You and I both know what fate has planned." Huginn and Muninn left St. Martin's body and landed on her shoulders. "If you want to change the future, you better ask for help, Dagrun Enemy of the Wolf."

She had to keep Arne safe. If she didn't, what would happen to their spark? She had no other choice.

So Dagrun did the only thing she could. She pushed herself to standing. "I'm over here!" she yelled into the soulless ice and snow.

"He's going to freeze out there by himself. In the cold, moonless, sunless gray."

They all were, Raven included. Dag, Arne, Frank and his concealed seer—everyone on Earth—all because the inevitability of the inescapable was going to kill her husband.

Huginn and Muninn flapped their wings against the blistering ice. "Bring help," she said to the birds. What choice did she have?

The birds vanished. Raven grinned. And the deal was set.

FAE TOUCHED

COMING SOON...

When the events surrounding the Samhain blizzard cause two dryads to come sniffing around Alfheim, Frank and Ellie are pulled into the center of a long-standing—and secret—battle between Arne Odinsson and Ellie's terrifying mother, Titania, Queen of the Fae.

FAE TOUCHED, Northern Creatures #5, available now.

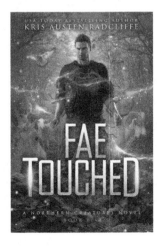

GET FREE BOOKS

SUBSCRIBE TO KRIS AUSTEN RADCLIFFE'S NEWSLETTER

Join my mailing list and receive **Pictures of You**, a Northern Creatures short story:

Left broken and grief-stricken after deadly magic rips away her best friend, an alluring stranger offers seer Ellie Jones the one thing she's never foreseen—hope.

PICTURES OF YOU

Magic moved the world. It started with a sway, then a rumble, then a twist in my guts as gravity moved sideways. I tried to speak. I tried to tell Chihiro—the one human who dared step across the boundary of my enchantments and extend her hand in friendship —to run. To turn away now and to never look back.

She realized what she was looking at the moment I handed her the photographic plate. She didn't need me to explain, or to point out where magic intersected with her reality.

Death stared back at my friend through the sepia tones of the daguerreotype in her hand. Death as a shadowy mist over what should have been a happy image of her placing a lovely, sweet-scented bouquet of magenta roses on my side table.

Death's hands signed the truth. Death's head floated over hers. Death would not leave her alone.

Chihiro Hatanaka, friend to a lowly, enchanted seer, was about to die....

Sign up for Kris Austen Radcliffe's Newsletter
www.krisaustenradcliffe.com

YOU WILL BE NOTIFIED when Kris Austen Radcliffe's next novel is released, as well as gain access to an occasional free bit of author-produced goodness. Your email address will never be shared and you can unsubscribe at any time.

THE WORLDS OF
KRIS AUSTEN RADCLIFFE

Smart Urban Fantasy:

Northern Creatures

Monster Born

Vampire Cursed

Elf Raised

Wolf Hunted

Fae Touched

Death Kissed

God Forsaken

Magic Scorned (*coming soon*)

Genre-bending Science Fiction about

love, family, and dragons:

WORLD ON FIRE

Series one

Fate Fire Shifter Dragon

Games of Fate

Flux of Skin

Fifth of Blood

Bonds Broken & Silent

All But Human

Men and Beasts

The Burning World

Dragon's Fate and Other Stories

Series Two

Witch of the Midnight Blade

Witch of the Midnight Blade Part One

Witch of the Midnight Blade Part Two

Witch of the Midnight Blade Part Three

Witch of the Midnight Blade: The Complete Series

Series Three

World on Fire

Call of the Dragonslayer (*coming soon*)

Hot Contemporary Romance:

The Quidell Brothers

Thomas's Muse

Daniel's Fire

Robert's Soul

Thomas's Need

Quidell Brothers Box Set

Includes:

Thomas's Muse

Daniel's Fire

Roberts's Soul

ABOUT THE AUTHOR

Kris's Science Fiction universe, **World on Fire**, brings her descriptive touch to the fantastic. Her Urban Fantasy series, **Northern Creatures**, sets her magic free. She's traversed many storytelling worlds including dabbles in film and comic books, spent time as a talent agent and a textbook photo coordinator, as well written nonfiction. But she craved narrative and richly-textured worlds—and unexpected, true love.

Kris lives in Minnesota with one husband, two daughters, and three cats.

For more information
www.krisaustenradcliffe.com

Made in the USA
Las Vegas, NV
16 September 2021

30451344R00125